VACATION

Vacation

DEB OLIN UNFERTH

McSWEENEY'S

SAN FRANCISCO

www.mcsweeneys.net

McSweeney's and colophon are registered trademarks of McSweeney's,
a privately held company with wildly fluctuating resources.

ISBN: 978-1-934781-09-8

In memory of John Kenneth Unferth (1965 2004)

Chapter One

CLAIRE

I recall only one sentence that she said. She said it all the time. Every day was an occasion. If she had to be away on a shoot, she said it to my father. If I had to take cough syrup, she said it to me. She said it to the family dog before his operation. It was her wisdom. She said it with pride. What my mother said was: You won't even feel it.

I was born in the city. My father was a bank man, my mother starred in soaps. We lived like the famous in a house by the park and I woke to a vase of fresh tulips each day. We had long hallways and long tablecloths. My mother had rooms full of clothes. So many strangers gave us presents that we had a man to pen our thank-yous. Photographers slept outside the house.

One day when I was five, my mother was hit by a car and she felt it and she died and we felt it. We went away for a while, paid off our debts from afar, tried to live without her. We came back to the city. My father's business spoiled dollar by dollar. We lived on her money. Each year we grew poorer. We sold the house and moved into a smaller house and then into a large rented apartment, then into a smaller one. We moved around the city, fitting into smaller and smaller spaces, each time carrying our valuables up and down stairways—the chests, the paintings, the family china, the sofas, the wardrobes. We finally landed in the smallest studio with the dog and our little cat and all of our furniture and light fixtures and jewelry. We laid out the expensive rugs one on top of another on the floor. We hung the paintings floor to low ceiling. It was in this room that my father became sick and couldn't work. We sold our things off one by one, peeled up a rug or took down a picture, and in this way we paid the medical bills and the other bills and we lived, somewhat. When the floor and walls were bare and the room was mostly cleared out, my father had one more thing to tell me. Early in our marriage, he said, your mother ran off with someone else and she came back pregnant. You are not my daughter.

I felt that too.

I was sixteen that year.

Today I thought about the man who raised me because of a man who sat down next to me on the train. He had a strangely shaped head. It seemed to be almost dented a little. He kept to himself on his seat and I to myself on my seat. We regarded one another.

Later I woke to an empty seat beside me and we pulled into the Syracuse depot. I looked out the window at the few frail people waiting for a train the other way, a strip of woman and her tiny, mittened girl. Suitcases on the bench. And there, I saw him, the man with the head. He'd gotten off the train. He was standing flush-faced in the chill, his suitcase on the platform, his hat crushed in his hand like a wad of paper, the other hand curled around the handle of a briefcase. A businessman. A man with a two-week vacation that he gets no matter what. If he dies and hasn't used his two weeks, they wrench open his coffin and put the money inside.

But who would want to waste a vacation on a place like that, a town so cold and so small, jammed into the countryside like a sliver? Part of a train ticket, an extra included in the fare, is that they'll move you even if you don't know where you are or how to get anywhere. If you are too exhausted or brainless, if your brain has been killed off and destroyed, if you are dead, they will still transport you, as long as your ticket has not expired. That's how that man looked at that moment with the splinter of Syracuse stuck in his head. He looked a little like the man I had called father most of my life—not the head, my father's was a perfect egg, but because he had the same false energy of someone who does not yet know they are down for the count. Then the train was pulling out. He followed it, first with his eyes, then with his body, turning as it went. I closed my eyes. I didn't want to see him left behind.

Chapter Two

The train pulled away. Myers walked the length of the platform.

He took a cab to Gray's neighborhood, lines of identical houses in rows, different from each other only in superficial ways—the size of the chimney or placement of the porch—or in meeker assertions, a mailbox that looked like a reindeer, a soggy doll fastened to a swing. Evidence of thoughtless, pleasureless lives.

The taxi pulled up to Gray's house. It was set back from the street and it sunk into the coming darkness. Shut blinds, an empty driveway, an unmowed lawn. The cabman put the car in park, swiped the meter. Myers stayed where he was.

They don't just spill onto the sidewalk, my friend, the cabman said. You go up and ring the bell. Ding dong.

Myers got out and ran up. It was raining here too and water went down his face. He rang and waited. No one came to the door. He flipped the mailbox. A full run of mail, side-stacked, stuffed. He rang again. He opened the screen and knocked. An ineffectual thud on solid wood. The house was the muted color of a people dominated by the landscape, people who just want to get something down that won't blow away. He knocked again, rapped on the diamond window. Through it, dark shapes, stillness. So Gray wasn't home yet. Okay. He grasped the doorknob, turned it (why not? the fucker), shook it. It was locked. He looked at his watch. Now what.

Under his feet the word WELCOME had its say.

He ran back to the taxi.

Where'd you come in from? asked the cabman, turning the meter back on, putting the car in park. Myers told him (wearily) and the cabman said he'd been there, damn fine locale, a bit busy, you know what, they put their garbage on the sidewalks and there's traffic, crime, parking's impossible, but nice spot. Then the cabman told him where he, the cabman, was from and also told him where his parents were from and where their parents were from and his wife's parents too, both sides and the sides before that. Then he went on to tell him about his daughter—age, eye color, favorite book this week, favorite book last week—then about his wife and the wife before this one, which one was better, in what ways. Then about the circles he drove in each day and what changes he noticed in them, in the cement and the paint and the people, the spread of Syracuse, the flat of it, all this and more, and how long did Myers want to wait?

Hi Gray, he was going to say. Thought I'd just drop in, see what you had going on here. Check in on the nearby alumni, sort of knock around. I see the kitchen could use a coat of paint. Maybe some new cabinets. Somebody should take apart that foosball table. How about if I give you a hand? Whatever's needed, whatever minor chore stands undone. Here, why don't you get up on this ladder, Gray, check the gutter—careful! Oh, oops. Hand me that hammer, would you? That saw? That power drill?

Lean over this way a little. I can't seem to get your eye from this angle.

Small satisfactions awaited him on the other side of these moments.

Was Gray a fix-it man? Did he own a foosball table? A ladder?

When Myers thought about it, he didn't know anything about the guy.

Outside, twig trees, half-empty, dim in last daylight, the day moving to night. A scratch of naked bushes. Inside, the cabman talked on and on, now about a radio he'd bought, now a trapeze artist he'd known, the three-finger waltz he'd learned from his ma, a knife he'd found on the backseat one day, not sharp enough to hurt anyone, a carving knife, like for clay, you understand, for reducing the size of sculptures, for making objects smaller, slowly.

Guy's not coming, he got around to saying at last.

He'll be here.

Meter's running.

I can see that.

He had to be around here somewhere. He still had his usual teaching schedule, four four, comp, business writing, a mild commute. Last time Myers had called (and hung up), Gray had still answered in his despondent voice at both phones—home and office—and there was no sign of anyone picking up and taking off midsemester. That much Myers felt certain of.

What's that you say? You don't know what this is about? Maybe a little drill in the earhole will jog your memory. Maybe a little claw of the old clawhammer to the knee. Maybe some takeout, as in, let's take this outside. As in, let's take your fingers outside, one by one, toss them out the window. Then let's see what you know and don't.

Small satisfactions and, who knows, maybe big ones too.

An hour was going by and then had gone by and another was beginning. Around them, the citizens of Syracuse were dragging themselves home from another day on the make. One got into a sport-utility vehicle two driveways down, his swollen body stuffed inside a coat and slouched under an umbrella. Myers himself was plumped under his own layers of cloth and plastic-based materials.

So what shot you off to Syracuse? the cabman was saying now.

Oh, the usual—vacation, fleeing the cubicle, you know, Myers said.

Odd spot for a holiday.

Friend of the wife.

I don't see a wife anywhere.

She's coming later.

The cabman seemed to have chatted himself out. Seemed ready for an explanation from the backseat, by God. He glanced back at Myers. The cabman, fore-armed, seamannish, ex-army. Myers was beginning to despise him.

How much longer you want to wait?

Give him a little, said Myers. Eye on the front door, the driveway, the walk.

I'm turning off the engine.

Leave it on. It's cold out.

He shut it off.

Hello Gray, good to see you. It's Myers. So you're still living alone, I see. Gained a few pounds, put on a few years, lost a hair or two, huh, pal? We sat in the same room for fourteen weeks running once. We gazed at numbers on a board. We bubbled in our Scantron sheets, put down our pencils when done. I suspect your grades were as middling as mine. Maybe worse—you're dumber. Remember the macaroni, the buttered toast? The jello salad? That's right, we ate food that came out of the same troughs. I missed my chance to gut you right then.

He had memories of Gray from college days. Gray had appeared some sophomore year and sat in the cafeteria with a backpack. He rifled through papers, scribbled, dog-eared, lined up his bottles of soda. After that he mostly vanished into the public transportation system—Myers recalled a glimpse of him leaning around the bus stop. Myers could remember no award of any sort being given the man. No sailing trophy, no honor roll, no debate club. No special interests, no reading *Mein Kampf* on the quad or passing out religious pamphlets, no part in any play.

What happened to your head anyway? said the cabman.

My head? Myers wiped his nose. Oh, I think I'm coming down with a cold.

Uh-huh.

Gray (he'd say, putting down his briefcase, propping an arm on the doorframe), I rode all the way from New York today. I had the worst day of my life. Six hours on a train will do things to a man. I feel like I've got a broken hip now. I feel like I've got a broken neck. And I'm tacked to all this suitcase crap. I have to tell you, Gray, for your sake I wish I had a broken neck, I really do. A man with a broken neck knows the thing is over. His enemies are safe. The way it stands now—I hate to say it—for you, it's not looking good.

The crew cut, the hard face, the cabman. I'm off soon, he said.

Myers could jimmy the door. After all, they had been classmates. It was better than riding all this way and not bothering to confirm he wasn't here. Better than going as far as the train, as far as the Syracuse depot, the cab, the curb, the mat, and then giving up, not even attempting the house itself. If anyone asked, came prowling by with a shotgun, he could say, Oh, he asked me to drop in, bring in the mail, water whatever stood it, that order of thing.

What else does Myers remember from those college days when Gray was around and Myers ignored him, just let the guy walk on by while Myers was wrapped up in his own bleak affairs, his own muddles? He remembered Gray's room had been next to the kid who sang on the balcony, the asshole who sang though he had no voice for it, and even if he had, nobody remembered buying a ticket and standing in line to hear any singing, so why did he have to let the whole building in free? Gray had often been half on the scene that way—accidentally present, nearby someone doing something.

In fact Gray had been the most unremarkable student the town had ever seen, and he went that way, unremarked on, through four years of auto-replay days of college and then two more for some other forgettable degree, a brief marriage, a quiet divorce. Myers had found all this out from his own unremarkable seat in front of the computer screen.

Myers hadn't been spectacular either. He did what he was best at: sat toward the front and took notes. He managed to secure a degree in two pointless subjects (Spanish, design), pointless because, well, he'd never spoken to an actual Spanish-speaking person who wasn't being paid for the pleasure. But he took care of his library fines, sleeved his degree in plastic, slogged away. That was the last he'd seen of Syracuse. He moved to Brooklyn, rode around on the train in a suit along with everybody else. Took one job, then another. Felt the panic of empty repetitive motion. Then one day he felt like he'd finally found a way to make it all worth waking up for, had met this amazing woman.

Myers might try this tack: Gray, I'll remove the shotgun from your mouth but you have to tell me what happened. I may not know you well but I've known you longer than I've known most humans alive. Longer than I've known my own beloved wife. She's left me at last. I mean, I've left her. I've agreed to go quietly or at least I've agreed to go. May as well, she's already left, in her way.

She had amazed him, all right, first by her sheer existence, then by agreeing to marry him, and then she kept amazing him further, he could never quite get over anything she did, he just stood there, stunned, until this very morning when he'd left, and she would probably amaze him more before it was done, yep.

It was night now. Outside, a car dome light spotlit a final woman tugging a grocery bag from a backseat and out into the pour. The color ran over the cement, the scrap of red purse, mud-yellow hair, bluish coat. Was that someone coming down the sidewalk? Too dark to see.

Other tiny college memories. Gray staring out the window of the library. Gray working the town video counter for a while. Had no car back then, could be seen walking, his head above the snowdrifts.

The cabman turned around in his seat, the headrest between them.

Is your wife really friends with this guy?

Oh, they have a special bond, all right.

You better not go near this guy, said the cabman, arm hooked over the seat. Whatever he did with your wife, it's over.

I don't want your advice.

It's not advice.

Just take me to a hotel.

My shift is over. Get out.

Hotel.

Out of the cab, buddy.

I'll need my suitcase.

He walked.

The hotel, the situation of the hotel, the predicament of it, out there on the outskirts of town, couldn't have been worse. All the hollow blocks, all the horizontal landscapes of his dreams. Somebody had come and flattened the earth down like this, as an intentional act, and then swept it clean of debris, put in these space-age cartons. This series of low-gravity chambers, a cheap trial run, a sample of the final made from chrome. It was the ugliest building of his life, a cluster of antennae and plates sticking off the roof, a few bleak balconies looking out over a wash rack of highways, a breeze chilling through. Strings of parked cars receded away into a dense thicket of lots.

So Gray hadn't come home. The lesson learned here was to not ever, ever look forward to anything, ever. Crush expectation. Count on nothing but your own grave. The only thing to do now was to check into this crap hotel, put his crap down, and emerge with a grimmer outlook.

His own smallness, his solitude, the cul-de-sac of his mind.

He'd asked her to marry him almost immediately on meeting her. He knew right away he would love her.

Places Gray might be: He might be standing on linoleum or carpet, his shoes in contact with it. Or he might not be standing. He might be lying down on soft sheets at this time of day, as in sleep, love, or illness. He might be next to a table, sitting at it. He might have his elbows on it. Or he might be in water, or falling through air toward it, diving. Pool, lake, ocean. Or it might have nothing to do with water, but there might be grass or trees or other markers suggesting nature.

Who could even imagine all the places Gray might be right now?

Not that the man had that much to leave. Look at this town. Myers had just walked through it in the rain. To get to this hotel.

But that's the way humans and objects roll over the earth, like water displacing other water. One human going this way with a few personal items in tow while another scoots off another way, and meanwhile the rain and the birds and the mountains falling to the ground, the pull of gravity tugging it all in, while things try to slide around to the left or right without banging into anything so hard that it might be smashed, or so softly that it might not be noticed.

The fact was that he was finding himself here and not where he had wanted.

The hotel rose overhead, a structure of plaster and dust, a few pieces of it torn away like an abandoned site. Strips of yellowing grass between parking lots. Above, the pinkish sky. Myers could be anywhere right now. Further proof of the great lack of imagination on the part of humanity: to look at the land and see the sameness that one sees in one's heart. No one should spend their life going through places like this. One's mind and soul may look like this, but to have to see it outside oneself was really just too much.

I'll need a room and a car, said Myers at the desk.
    That's fine.
    I'll need the car tonight.

He rolled his suitcase down the corridor. Would go back tonight and wait Gray out. The guy would have to show up sometime. At least in the morning. Sometime he would have to come home and brush his teeth.
    Suitcase. It contained belongings like all belongings, removed from the premises of his home, placed in a trunk, and then that rode on the rack across the state. Just pieces of cloth, cut, dyed, arranged, and sealed together with thread to approximate the shape of his body. Folded and stapled papers, such as his passport (in case of a trip to Niagara Falls— look out, Gray! don't lean over the edge), laptop...

I'm checking in. I've checked in. I'm in a hotel. Like a vacation.

A vacation, his wife said.

Yes. Of sorts.

(She made a sound.)

What was that?

What?

That noise.

That was laughter. It expresses mirth.

What is so goddamn funny?

You on vacation.

Why is that funny?

You never take vacations.

Yes, I do. I do all the time.

You go see your parents twice a year.

Wife. Here is an index of all the words he had read aloud to her from letters, books, menus during their year of courtship and nearly three years of marriage. Here is an abridged list of random thoughts he'd had before drifting off to sleep any old night during these four years they'd spent together. Here is a list of the trips they'd taken, together or apart, the number of nights each of them had spent outside the New York metro area since meeting. Here is a list of items purchased. Here is a list of the gifts they'd given each other on holidays, in chronological order, then in order of most appreciated, least disliked. Here is a list of the times each had said the other's name, and the times they'd had sex, arranged into groups by position, then entered into a ledger in order of duration, in order of urgency, first to last, best to worst.

She slipped through crowds, spoke softly, never screeched, but somehow could always be heard. He loved that about her. Even her applause was understated. She had thin hands.

The hotel room itself was worse, some sort of misunderstanding between human and machine, a mistake about the meaning of the word "clean." A "fresh" smell like poison gas, or a scent intended to lure and trap and kill. Or about the meaning of "convenient," contraptions bolted into walls and tables as if built by an alien tribe based on descriptions read from dictionaries—lamp, remote control, pencil cup—so that it looked like a reconstruction by someone who had never seen the original. It looked like the entire container could be picked up and carried off at any moment without rattle or disarray, could be tossed into the trash without any pieces flying out. A habitat for the human creature, a replica, a "house" that could be hosed down and ready in a minute should the human die off and need replacement.

I take vacations.

You don't like going anywhere.

I'm on vacation right now.

No, you're not.

I'm in a hotel room, aren't I? You don't believe me? Call the front desk and ask.

Being in a hotel room does not mean you're on vacation. I can think of plenty of reasons why someone might be in a hotel room and not on vacation.

Like what?

Funeral.

Oh sure, blame it on the dead.

Divorce.

That could count as a vacation.

Divorce does not count.

It could.

It does not.

The business center downstairs was another insult to recover from, another bland cage he thrust himself into, a place based on a belief in beige. As if the inhabitants were insane and needed soothing, or as if they had underdeveloped brains and could only register simple images, stick figures in place of words. Remain calm. Go this way in case of sudden, violent emergency. And perhaps he was such an inhabitant. Perhaps so.

I could take a vacation if I goddamn well felt like it.

You're not on one now.

Damn well could be.

But you're not. And what happened to your—what did you call him? oh, yes—your "friend"?

He's, well, he's...

I have to go. I have a meeting in the morning.

I bet you do.

He sat down at a terminal. His email lit up the screen, mass-market mud filled his box. Amid it he noticed, suddenly, one in particular. A message floated up from its waterlogged porthole, shed of its cellophane.

A miracle.

He had an email from Gray.

Myers! What a surprise. In from the city? Of course I remember you. How could I forget a man with a head like yours? Sorry to have missed you. You should have called first. I'm on vacation, my friend, in the land of my dreams, the most beautiful country in the world—Nicaragua, of all spots to see the sun. I had to get out of there. That town is a saddle on a wild stag. Have fun in Syracuse. Decay away! If you can break a window and crawl over glass, my place is yours.

Gray

Myers walked to reception.

You can cancel the car, he said.

Chapter Three

Myers woke alone on the sofa.

This had been early that morning.

His wife was moving around in the kitchen. She had become the most efficient human being he'd ever known. She'd developed into this in the past few years, from someone who once could barely bother to open a bill.

The day was invading through the windows and under the doors. Dust floated in on a slant. He tugged at the couch cushion under his head.

She called to him. I think I'm going to go stay with Anita for a few days while I look for a place, she said.

He suddenly remembered the night before.

God, fucking Anita! he thought.

No, you are not going to go stay with fucking Anita, he called back.

(Anita, the high school friend, now nearly neighbor.)
(The takeout was still in the warmer.)
From the kitchen: I'm going to phone her and ask.

He went into the kitchen.

You are not going to go stay with Anita or whoever else.

I see you got takeout.

Yes.

You left it to burn in the warmer. You could have told me last night you bought dinner. Telling me in the morning is buying breakfast, burned breakfast.

I never liked that woman.

Failing that, you could have put it in the fridge.

She was standing there in a nightgown he'd always found appealing, a straight black affair with a bit of fringe at the bottom.

Failing that, you could have tossed it out, she said.

It doesn't matter. I'm leaving. You can stay.

Failing that, you could have not bought it.

He threw the takeout in the garbage. A substance like tar spilled from the carton.

Sleeveless, ribboned, stubborn. His wife.

Fine, leave, she said. Where are you going to go, by the way?

Yes, the night before they had finally agreed on a separation after he didn't know how many times they'd discussed it. It seemed like they'd been discussing it for years.

Her moving out was the best thing she could do for their marriage, they'd decided.

Can anybody imagine what that might mean? Does that make any sense whatsoever? No.

It was the best possible course of action, considering, they'd agreed.

24

They'd each be fine once they settled in. Almost nothing would change. They'd each keep taking the subway in their triangles or squares or walking in them. Leaving would be hard, no question. Leaving is a large dog blocking the way of the exit. But it would all work out. They were joined, after all, just by paper, mostly, and by awkwardly shaped pieces of wood, porcelain, glass, metal, bits of cloth, ideas about soap, beliefs about historical events, sleeping habits, memories of rainfalls and other watery things (oceans, ponds, faucets) that they had visited or seen together in pictures.

She leaned in. I see you've made it all the way to a suitcase, she said.

He had a pile of shirts there.

Do you have a destination or are you just going to flap your arms and hope you hit something safe?

I'm going to see someone. Don't look for an apartment.

Who?

A friend.

What friend?

You've never met him. (This was true, technically.)

What friend of yours haven't I met?

From college.

What friend do you have from college?

One you've never met.

Don't you have to work?

I'm taking vacation time.

You're not eligible for vacation time yet.

The suitcase was open on the bed. A brown zipper carry-on.

Socks and so forth. Two-ply.

Yes, the job was new and an issue.

Gray was—who knows—lifting and lowering a cup, tying on a shoe for another unhappy contention with the outdoors. Gray, upright, at home (also gray, perhaps).

Don't you think you need a plane ticket to go somewhere? she said.

Don't you think you need to let your boss know that you're planning to not show up?

Don't you think you need to let this "friend" know you're coming?

You're not taking the car, she said. If you had any ideas like that.

She stood there, tapping her foot.

You could take the train, she said.

Items to divide, clutch, abandon, or destroy: Items that looked like animals but weren't—the duck pitcher, the turtle placemats. Flat items or items with flat sides—bookshelves, nightstands. She would just move over a little, that's all, to a new spot, her spot.

(...had agreed at last and then he had spent the night at the window, his wife gone to bed...)

And no, he was not going to take the car. What did she think, he was going to drive to his vacation? What sort of holiday is that, dealing with traffic tickets and gas stations and flats? No, he'd dropped the friend an email. The friend would pick him up at the train.

He'd sent this friend an email?

Sidekicked it. Into his box.

He'd written the email, sent it, received an email back, and he was now telling her the accurate information contained in it?

He was going to do it. He was about to.

So he hadn't actually sent an email.

He hadn't gotten to it. What with this suitcase all over the place.

Oh, she sees.

He'll do it, he'll do it.

Her, with her eyebrow. Skirt, hem. Why doesn't he do it now.

All right, all right. He left the suitcase sitting there all over the place.

The way that man went (he could see it, Gray, walking over a vast expanse, past piles of bricks and under bridges, over cracked earth and broken stems and shingles)...

Or Gray, clothed, indoors, a frozen likeness.

Hey Gray, he typed. Yes, he had the email address. *Haven't seen you forever. Remember me, from undergrad? Thought it time for a talk. I'm headed your way. Taxi, train, taxi, that's the plan. Arrival at your place with a suitcase. That sort of day. Nothing to worry about. A few days off. Rest. Old friend, new conversation. I'll explain when I get there.*

Myers

He looked at it. He heard her back in the kitchen. He sent it.

There were also the mirrors, the photos, and other inaccurate reflections. The razor, the bathtub. The kids and the dog, although they had none. The idea of dog, that. The possibility of dog that now would not be possible. Her mother, or her mother's dislike of him, who would get that? Surely that would come with him. Along with the rooster clock that she loved, that he hated, that she bought when she started to hate him.

He could admit to being difficult in this last hour. The clutter on the bed and in his mind was like a pile of timber, shaved planks. But she was worse. She really made the thing impossible:

1. arguing with him when he asked for a ride to the train (couldn't be bothered to drive her husband to the train, he said, well, maybe he couldn't be bothered to go) and, after her finally agreeing,
2. refusing to bring the car around so that he had to carry his

belongings three blocks—his suitcase, his laptop briefcase, his raincoat, his overcoat (in case of actually arriving at his destination, the coldest, bleakest spot on the earth, a town that should be torn off and tossed), umbrella...

3. not popping the trunk for him (what, did she expect him to put everything down, find his keys, open the trunk, pick everything up—his overcoat slipping to the (wet) ground—while she sat in the driver's seat with the heat on? Not today, lady. Pop the trunk!) so that each step of what should have been an easy affair took a long time, then,

4. not driving him to the door of the station, insisting on letting him off at the end of the block on the other side of the street,

5. citing traffic,

6. citing the right turn she claimed to have to make, though she could have gone straight,

7. (she adjusted a barrette in the rearview)

8. citing the time,

9. –

Fact: She hadn't always been like this. She'd been warm, she had loved him.

They sat in the car on the corner.

So long then, was the line he was taking.

Have a good trip.

Up ahead, the station looked like an imprint on the sky, or perhaps done in stencil, colorless, two-dimensional.

At the ridiculous wedding she had loved him. In the new overapplianced apartment she had loved him, amid all those packages and boxes and houses of Styrofoam and glass. She had touched his face when he was tired, when he'd had another bad day at the office. He remembered that, the way she used to do that, the way she expected nothing back, it was gentle. As a nice rain. It had been there, it had drizzled. He recalled it with clarity. And the image hurt him, felt less like a drizzle than like an actual cutting into his brain, a piercing, bleeding. She had arrived as one thing and now, as he parted, she was another, some strange folded-up broken thing—and at the least he had done nothing to stop it and at the most he had caused it all.

I'll be back in a few days. I'll bring you something.

Not necessary.

A snow globe?

Fine.

A holiday T-shirt.

Whatever you like.

I'm going now.

Does it seem like it to you?

The station before them, sketched on, or stamped to a backdrop.

Don't look for a place until I get back. Will you do that one thing?

There's traffic, she said.

Sure, of course. The cars behind us, the assholes in the cars behind us, are more important than your husband—

They're honking.

People who work hard at, say, lifting heavy objects or running in sand or covering sheaves of paper with printed letters or pushing rocks around or up hills, they speak of it, they know how this feels, the miles of frustration, the weeks.

She'd always had this lonely air to her, and Myers, who'd had his own solitary life, had always felt protective. She was emotionally unmoored. A couple of times a year her parents came through and she grew sullen. She and Myers endured a few uncomfortable meals, answered their questions politely, let them pick up the bill exactly every other time. He did this with her even after she'd begun behaving the same brooding way with him.

Gray, stooped, leaning. Myers imagined him. Feet on floor wax maybe, walking up an aisle of desks—no, of laundry detergents, softeners. His feet and the floor, the shoes of him. Myers tracked the steps.

There was no proof anywhere, nothing he could point to except certain stretches of pavement, certain stop signs and traffic lights. Photos of the scene would show nothing but figures and moisture and streets. The prints were washed away years ago. But she knew and he did too what went wrong. She went wrong. She wronged, was wrong.

He should have taken care of this years ago. It was pride that had kept him from it. That and the belief that everybody would go back to their starting places, sulk or weep or whatever was needed, time would pass, the sharp pain lessen to a livable ache. But that hadn't happened. Everyone had coasted back to their corners, yes, and believe him, Myers had kept a toehold in just who was where and with whom, but time had dulled nothing, had only made it worse. He couldn't look at her without thinking of him and he couldn't be nice to her and he couldn't tell her about it or demand some answers and this was the state of things.

Last piece of her: palm, purse, thigh. He got out, watched her turn her face away, the car pull out into traffic. Gone.

None of their family members were buried in the same graveyard. He had often said how when he and she were laid out together, as they planned, it would be the first true joining of the families. Gross, she said.

Chapter Four

Had Myers done anything wrong or was everything her fault?

Everything?

Okay, there was the following. That one thing. He used to follow her.

Around the house?

Outside, on the street.

Where?

Wherever.

Like a stalker?

Not like a stalker. She's his wife.

People stalk wives. No wonder she threw him out.

She didn't throw him out, for God's sake. Did you see him back there? He left, he woke up and said he was leaving. Besides, she didn't know. She never knew about the following.

She might have known.

No.

Still, a thing like that affects.

What was he supposed to do, let her promenade all over the city in her stockings without him?

That's the way it works these days.

Not any way Myers knows of.

There's a word for it.

No word Myers ever heard of.

Employment?

Oh, that. Don't make him laugh.

In fact, he started following her in the first months of their marriage or thereabouts. Maybe month three. About two and a half years ago. Their normalcy back then was stunning and thorough. It wasn't this fun house he lived in now—distorted images, trapdoors, a lurching car. Back then they went to work, they came home. Sometimes they rode the train together, he carrying her bag. Sometimes they stayed in the city for a fish dinner, their favorite stools-and-counter spot. They made love, ironed. They discussed their belongings and the positions their belongings held, both in their esteem and in the apartment. And he hoped it would always be this way, marriage, adding more objects, subtracting a few, making love a little less but still frequently. Each day he came home elated, astounded by his luck. This graceful brilliant woman, this beautiful adorable creature loved him, of all people. He had not been a happy man before. He was determined not to mess this up.

One day she had called his office to say she'd be late. That's how it all started. He'd had a different job back then, a worse one, one that never required he stay late, and she'd had an even worse one, one that didn't require her at all. So when she said, I'm going to be late, it was surprise that her job needed her that made him say, Do you have to?

It's work, I'm working. I'm sorry. Order without me.

Order. He and his wife ate items that answered to a call, that were called for, items that arrived in foil with a plastic hat on top, the entire assembly placed into kraft paper, stapled for security, and then put inside an additional thin plastic bag tied at the top.

On that particular day, he forgot to ask which item she wished to find at the bottom of all the protective coverings. His mind that day was distracted, frayed from the longstanding understanding he had with walls, billboards, disembodied voices. No parking here to corner. Close-out deals now. Don't forget your lotto. Stand clear of the closing doors, please. He called back. She didn't answer her office phone or her cell. At the front desk they said she'd left an hour before.

The truth was, he could imagine a scenario where he would have to confess each time he followed her, one by one, would have to produce the date, hour, coordinates, trajectory. She would also confess her end of it, which was substantial. They would take turns, reciting sites and times, alphabetically or chronologically, marking them off one by one or deleting them from an electronic file.

She came home late that night, had something else in her or on her, a mussed appearance, a healthy ruddy complexion, not the dried tired look of someone with an evening of input and printout behind her. She had a callous glow.

Where were you?

I told you. Work.

Considering at that point she had never lied to him before, he didn't think.

I'll be late again, sorry. This was her calling again the next day.

If you say so.

I have to stay and work.

Duty gums the shoe, as they say.

What?

I'm just saying.

The slate of his brown desk, the planes and circles scattered over his screen, the uncoil of the phone cord. He rose, walked fourteen blocks in winter sun. Stood outside the building that did not but was supposed to contain her, stood beside a fountain of cement. He looked up, saw nothing, saw lit and darkened windows. The moral grid of steel spired up the side.

That, a hard man would count as the first night he followed her.

That time, of course, he didn't get very far and he didn't see her.

What could he do that night other than not sleep, wake dull, proceed as expected outwardly?

So she had lied and sneaked, a fact he could hardly get his head around.

Reasons not to confront her: (he couldn't think of any).

Reasons not to confront her: he couldn't believe it.

So she had lied about staying late at work. And she lied again when she came home. And she lied again the next day, and once more when she came home.

She hadn't been raised by warm people. Her father had a phony laugh. Her mother was prim, airtight, walked around looking cheated. The two of them appeared every other season, perched on their seats as if slightly offended by their surroundings and who was in them, and then melted back into the Midwest. Myers thought sadly of his wife as a little girl being raised among these people and forgave her own distanced, lonely air.

She called again. Would be late.

He ran the fourteen blocks, five of them long, nine short, because no way, wherever she thought she was going, she wasn't. He ran, sifting through the baby carriages, the shoppers, pushing if he had to, because what is worse, to knock someone over or miss the chance to stop her flat?

These were the sky-white winter days of inventory-clearance, streetside flea markets, sidewalk racks.

(It was the only time he had to run. After that he strolled, arrived early. In the spring, which fell upon them grimly with its hellish green, he ate a hot dog and waited for her to come down. She had dispensed with the calls to his office by that time, in any case.)

But that day he ran, pushing people out of the way. Let them fall over. Let them arrest him. Put him away. This disregard for the safety and comfort of others may be shocking but it was not as much of a shock as what he got just as he came tearing into the plaza—

She emerged from the building, walked right by.

In the past week they'd talked over meals and at bedtime about couch sizes, store names, power strips...

She didn't see him, didn't look his way at all. He froze, could not move. In the air, a border scratched between them.

...trivia (origin of the beanbag, sea-foam features, name of the world's greatest dolphin trainer), summer trips (beach, forest, falls?).

Her bag swung by her side. The light didn't light up anything special, didn't pick her out of the crowd. It lit what was there without expression, without distinguishing itself in any way other than the obstinacy of its own existence. Even the metal buckle on her bag, holding it all together so the mess didn't tumble out, the sunlight didn't shine on it that Myers could see, and he could see a lot from where he stood that day. He really could.

She was just a woman walking up the street..

He did not go after her, did not run down the long shadow of the sidewalk, swing her around by the arm. He stepped back, watched. People got around each other and into the space between them. The woman who lied walked away, did not yet know she'd been caught.

That he counted as the second day he followed her.

Other seconds: helpings, hands, rates, but mostly having to do with time, the time it took for one thought to follow another (her, her, her), and other followings, such as heartbeats, blinks, steps. Many of them added together or separated. He felt them. Not the minutes, mind you, but the seconds.

The next time, he was there and he followed. She went off. The background blurred in his eye. She stopped, sat on a bench on the loudest corner the earth had ever known. A catastrophe of buses and drillings, the dash of the taxi, the rush and halt, the tamping down of the cement, the suck of air in, the press of it out, the slow sink of the city, the spread of tar, the lifting of it, the footsteps going through, the out and out of breaths. He watched. In front of him two children knocked around a construction cone.

Who the hell did she think she was, sitting there like that?

She jumped up and was off again, walking over the invisible shake of the train, through the lines of cars standing at traffic lights. She turned into a restaurant. He followed her in, had to do some sidestepping to get in there around the sizing-up going on. A place as bland as anywhere— some sort of cheap, meaningless theme of boats or vegetables or body parts on the walls, their tin representations glowing and flaking. A tune pumped in. Food descending onto tables. People much like himself and herself in suit get-ups and in various conversational postures—lovey, feigning, shrill. He couldn't find her. He pushed through the hands reaching and retracting.

He found her. She was alone at a small round table. She sipped something from a mug. She sat for an hour, doing nothing. Staring.

If she was meeting someone here, he was late.

If she was meeting someone here, he wasn't meeting her.

She stood up at last. Myers bowed into the bathroom to avoid her. He went out to the street and she was gone.

This was so early in their marriage that they still had packing materials around, half-empty boxes, silver in sleeves, Styrofoam noodles. The apartment felt huge when she wasn't there, too white. It was so early in their marriage he still believed he knew her, that he could. He still believed in that—knowing.

She complained about work. The meetings were long and tedious, she said. She fell asleep in her chair, she said. She nearly fell out the window she was so bored. She nearly leapt, that's how bad it was, you can't imagine. She would have welcomed an earthquake.

All the extra work they were giving her, she said. Unpaid hours, late meetings, she hadn't eaten dinner, her feet were sore, her eyes, her very head was vacant, depleted of thought, canceled, zeroed out. That's how tired she was.

His rage was a saw, going back and forth, cutting through arteries, hers. They had a dinner of steam-table vegetables, ate quietly across from one another. They slept. Or rather, she slept. Or acted like she did.

Reasons not to confront her: clearly the woman was not in the mood to tell him the truth about any subject larger than a button. And he himself had no intention of showing his shapes too soon.

He followed her. For weeks this went on. Sometimes he managed to track her all the way home and then he had to make up excuses, dissimulate (because he never actually lied, he was sure), invent where he'd been. She met no one, spoke to no one, maybe a word to a server or cashier. Her movements were random, jumpy. One minute sitting, staring into a mass of tables, the next rising, heading for the door, a few dollars down for the bill. He couldn't understand it. She didn't read or write or eat. She drank tea or coffee. Or just stood outside, often the same nondescript building flung up in front of her, her bag slouching her shoulder. She lied like an adolescent when she came home. What could he say? He knew she was going for walks? He wasn't saying a thing until he found out just what she thought she was getting away with.

Was she getting crazy, perhaps? Crazier?

Reasons not to confront her: who was she now?

He wrote her letters, rewrote, revised, tore them up.
1stly I saw you exit the building and turn right.
2ndly I saw you go four blocks.
3rdly I saw you on the next corner stop in front of a store window and not look into it, a store you adore. As your husband, I know.
4thly I saw you cross the street, stop, then cross back again.
5thly why did you do that? There was nothing ahead and nothing behind. Coming darkness, filled avenues.
6thly I saw you walk east again.
7thly I saw you pass the spot of original departure and continue.
8thly I saw you turn left onto Broadway and pass through a heavy crowd of tourists.

9thly why did you do that? You hate that.
*10thly why didn't you turn at any point and see me? You never even looked
    left or right.*
11thly what happened to you after that? I lost you.
12thly what's the matter with you?
13thly I saw you keep moving but I couldn't get through.
14thly when did you stop?

About the lights: He knew about the lights, that they had become an issue, in place of The Issue, that the lights had become a stand-in or substitute, as they are for sunlight or moonlight. He knew they had this additional function, they obscured as well as brightened, were a deflecting glare where before there had been none, only voices, cool rooms, he knew he and she had achieved this when one day he came home and said, Why are all these lights on?

(Question: who cares?)

She was sitting on the couch, watching TV. She looked up and said, There are three lights on.

She named them: 1. the kitchen, 2. the hallway, 3. the living room.

Why do you need the one on in the kitchen?

To get a drink.

And the hallway?

To walk to get a drink.

You need a light on for that?

Yes, I do.

And in here? (After all, she had the goddamn TV.)

To sit in the spot where the drink will be drunk.

It wasn't only the lights that acted as a detour. Other subjects and objects did as well. There was the tea and the issue about that. There was the garbage and all of that. The laundry, her laundry, and what she did with it, and his laundry and what he did with it. And all the other items that got scuffed or hung up or needed dealing with, floors and hangers and checkbooks. There was her slow-moving tone and his, slowly moving from loving to harsh, the slow movement of them moving away from each other on the bed.

She could be taking a walk, a series of walks, as exercise or for temperament or temperature regulation. She could be looking for something she lost, a valuable coin, an earring. She could be sad, require air, pavement. She could be pacing—not in her own home but out-of-doors, a cityscape pacing. She could be searching, not for something lost but for something not yet seen. Or she could be searching for a way to tell him, she could be looking for a brink to be on, or an edge to be off. She could be feeling too prominent, like the most prominent object in any scene, she could be fleeing that, wanting diminishment, wanting extraction, to be taken out of any given situation. Where could she walk to that she wouldn't be?

She could be merely avoiding him? She could be taking the long way home?

It is ridiculous, he said, to have three lights lit and only one person.

Two people.

I only just arrived.

How do you know I wasn't leaving on anticipatory lighting?

We're both in the same room.

How was I supposed to know where you'd want to be? she said. Maybe I should have left the bedroom light on. Maybe I should have lit the back porch. Maybe I should have left on anticipatory lighting for me because I should have anticipated that you'd come home and carry on at me and I'd have to get up and leave the room.

Which she did.

And he followed.

That was the first month he followed her. So each weekday evening, that's twenty, plus a few mornings, maybe twenty-five total the first month. He could apologize for each of those, if she would, like hearing or telling the same story twenty-five times. And she just might. But there wasn't going to be anything fun in it. She may as well know that right up front.

There she was, his wife, walking under a string of awnings.

She said the cost was minimal and he said the issue wasn't cost but waste. She said the waste was minimal and he said yes, but existent. She said she didn't want to sit in the dark and he said then she should certainly have a light on. One light. And if she went into another room she should turn out that light and turn on the one in the other room. She said he was being a bully. She said she'd had a hard day. She was so tired. She said he should just leave, go someplace else where he could be in the dark. He said, for God's sake, could they not fight? Could she just sit quietly beside him? And she said he could sit quietly in the dark by himself. She screamed it a little, You can goddamn well sit quietly in the dark by yourself. And he swung open the back door that let out to the landing (sudden cool air), screamed, Fine, I'm leaving! walked out, walked eight blocks (black branches against red sky), turned, went back.

There were the considerations of the bladder. Also of the stomach. Thirst. The organs had to be taken into account. The feet.

What the hell was she doing?

Now look, I know you weren't at the office, he said.
    She startled from her fuzzed fruit.
    Of course not. We met over dinner with a client.

Where?

Why are you asking?

Why won't you say?

Why are you badgering me?

His wife, spooned hand, rising from her seat.

This is what was going on within the plaster of their home during the months of him behind her and her never turning around, never wondering whether her own husband kept better track of his own wife than to let her toddle off down the cement. What kind of man did she suppose she had banished herself to and what kind of wife had he wound up with, a nutcase?

There she was, walking along the dark rim of Chinatown. Stopping. Her feet on the round of a manhole cover. Then going on.

Are you badgering me for any particular reason? she said. Are you referring to anything that has ever been in contact with this household before? Or did that question fly in from outside?

Is there something you want to say to me that could be an accusation or a threat? she said.

Because if so, please do, she said. Let's see this fault of mine. Where is it?

Woman-walker, slack-rope artist, shilly-shallier.

Where is it? she said.

Myers—anyone could have seen him there, enclosed within paint, insulation, flooring, and ceiling, a wife with one hand raised in exasperation, her mouth opening and closing.

Well? she said. The whole paper caboodle of city hung on the sky behind her.

Well? she said.

Anyone could have seen him not say.

Chapter Five

The regional manager had many interesting questions.

What happened to you yesterday? Was it a magic trick? A sleight of hand? Did you forget to pull yourself out of a hat? I don't need to tell you this is not the finest time for fun.

Myers, in Syracuse, one arm running the length of the hotel room desk.

Where's Myers today? I said to everyone. Does anyone see him pushed up against a wall around here? Did he get stuck in a manila envelope?

I should have called sooner, Myers said. I'm in the wrong there. The important thing is we're speaking now.

The regional manager made many interesting statements.

The important thing is yesterday's absence and the ibid of that today and the fact that my caller ID is showing me a number which does not match the number of your office phone and of which I do not recognize the area code. That is the important event in your life today.

Yes, I need to talk to you about that, said Myers.

Now's the time. The world over awaits.

I'm taking a vacation day.

What vacation. You've been in our employ four months. You don't get any vacation. You get vacation in August.

I'm taking one yesterday and one today. (Myers looked at his watch.) And one tomorrow.

You want, you take vacation in August. You apply for it. Like everyone does. You submit a form six weeks in advance. We plan for your absence.

Melanie can mind my work.

Melanie cannot mind your work. Melanie is busy minding Melanie and Melanie's work.

I'm taking a sick day, in that case.

What sick days. You take sick days when you're sick. So which is it—are you sick or are you on vacation?

I'm both, said Myers. Listen. It's both. I'm leaving my wife.

In the first month Myers followed her, they fought about light switches as well as lights. Dimmers, three levels. They fought about seven different things having to do with bicycles. They fought about round tin objects, lids, water, other liquids, other things having to do with liquid, with containers. She said they fought about everything.

He said, Not so. There was plenty they didn't fight about.

See? Even that he had to contradict.

I'm sorry to hear that, Myers. Really I am. The best thing you can do is to keep your seat belt on, as they say. High hat the hell hole. Eyes to the front, and so on. Shoot the face of misfortune.

She's moving out.

Excellent. Better off without her, I say. No offense. Take moving day off. Listen, make moving day on the weekend. Make moving day next month. Let her move herself. We need you here this week. It's a mess in here. You've got your own project. Projects.

I've already left.

Don't tell me things I can see, Myers. My eyes are on your vanished form over your desk. Where are you? Where are you phoning from?

Syracuse.

That's no vacation. That's a smudge.

To be accurate, they had not fought about most things.

They had not fought about the shape of certain objects, never disagreed about whether an object was round or tall. They had not fought about the outlines of things, how it worked so that one thing could be separated from another, what occurred to mark the division atomically. They had not fought about any of Newton's laws or Kepler's laws or whoever was in charge these days, whoever had won. They agreed on up and down and how that worked and how to trigger it. The nonsubstance of shadows, the substance of what the shadows were shadows of. They agreed on God-related issues (there is no God, they believed) and on all that follows (no barricading oneself in or jaunting off somewhere to upset or placate a jealous God) (no floating up and down like balloons) (no Body moved anything first or was there before anybody else). They agreed on many practical truths: Mathematics seems to work fairly well, they thought, as do the languages, with a few garbage alleys of misunderstanding. The social sciences, such as psychology, have their place but it's tiresome to discuss them, especially Freud.

They even agreed on some aspects regarding lights—the way they work, the hardware, their function, etc.

What kind of man behaves this way? she said.

I mean, who did he think he was?

I mean, what was he supposed to be? A husband?

Let me tell you, husbands aren't supposed to act this way.

Myers, are you there? Myers.

Yes.

I'm not a difficult man, am I?

No, you're not.

We give the standard allowances and perks. Discount parking, yes?

I take the subway.

I don't try to be an asshole.

No, you don't.

You've put me in a difficult situation here. You've been working on the Smithson journals. This is a new account, your first project. You have been entrusted with this. You have been the point man. Anything to do with Smithson, you are pointed at, and you, in turn, point elsewhere. What is the point of having a point man I can't point to? No one else knows what is happening with Smithson. Smithson is due the day after tomorrow so it is obviously no good for you to come back the day after tomorrow. Where are the files? Are the files on your laptop?

(Yes.)

I always bring my work home with me, sir.

Do we have backups here?

(The backups were in his briefcase.)

Safe in my briefcase, sir.

What is the point of having files I don't have?

I don't mean to drop the ball on this.

You are throwing the balls out the window. You are throwing other things out the window. Reputations. Money. Jobs—your job. Now, today. Today is a bad day. Today you are in Syracuse. I want you to pack up that laptop, get on an airplane, and come back to New York. That's going to be expensive. Same-day fare, few direct flights. I will pay for it. That is my gift to you, my condolence card for your breakup. Get to the airport, come home, come here. Tonight you will stay in a hotel. On us. On me. Dinner too. With me. Bring your laptop. We are here for you in your time of need. Are you hearing this, Myers?

I am.

Good, see you this afternoon.

Okay, sir.

Don't call me sir. Call me by my name.

Myers hung up. He sat in the protective circle of light formed by the hotel and by the present itself and these shone above him and around him but illuminated nothing. He called the front desk.

I'll need a taxi to the airport, he said.

On Gray: Here is a fact Myers couldn't know or even suspect. At the same moment Myers struck out down the hall for the elevator, suitcase rolling behind, Gray was elsewhere thinking, You know, that Myers fellow could be of some use just now. Gray was far away, stepping over a pockmarked Central American topography. He paused, considered the arrangement of gravel under his feet. The sun soaped the clouds. He pulled some coins from his pocket, turned them over on his hand. Myers slid in and out of his mind like a bird in and out an open window. He went on.

Gray had had few thoughts of Myers in his life. The first ones had been as a student. He'd observed Myers's head from the back of the room and studied its odd contours—not outrageous, but irregular. No one knew why. In the dorms the guys discussed whether he'd been in an accident or if it was the result of some sort of careful genetic planning. They were beyond teasing and no one wanted to ask. Myers had no close friends. From some angles the head appeared normal. Such as straight on. If Myers looked in the mirror each day he wouldn't see anything strange at all. The guys gradually realized he wasn't aware of it. This was interesting and Gray pondered it in class, but it was only one of many drifting thoughts: girlfriend (gum-chewing), dormmates (loud), the qualities of light in the room (daylight here, fluorescent there), the square of a morning toast, a skyscraper he'd seen in a dream.

Thus Gray engaged himself through geometry.

He received a C in the class and for the next six years Gray had no thoughts of Myers. He finished one degree and began and finished another. He married the mintmouth girlfriend and settled down in Syracuse, though he'd never lived anyplace else. He shifted from the back of the room to the front, turned around, gathered papers instead of writing them, faced whichever direction he was pointed with the same dejection, went home and sat through her dejection, back and forth like that until nearly three years ago when he left, finally.

Before they split for good there was a lot of talk about resorts—not as in sunshine and sea, but as in "last resort"—and Gray and his wife tried them all: time apart, time together, compromise, birthday presents.

Those are normal, said Gray's father on the phone, who was, after all, an informed man. You do those anyway.

Therapy too.

Normal.

It was like talking to a telemarketer.

Telemarketers are normal.

Yeah, she had her script all right.

She or the therapist?

Both. It was like talking to two telemarketers.

That's normal.

So the marriage was over and both sides were banged up about it, but even more they seemed to have a small child from the thing, a girl. It had not yet been decided how that portion would divide up, what days would be his, how often he would see her, whether he would get a holiday and which, and Gray felt worse about that piece of it being broken off and floated away. It was something to try not to think about. She was. His weanling, his springling, his sprout.

Myers. In Syracuse. The hotel called him a cab and he made it to the airport. He went in, confronted the place, its identical hallways, identical chairs, mirrored metal, the sort of place that inspires panic, requires spellbound acceptance. He had the fact of a suitcase to hold onto, and his other clutter, hat and so on, coats. He maneuvered around the right-angle objects placed in his path—counters, windows, walls. The floor speckled the floor.

So three years ago Gray and his wife split. Who wanted to leave whom had not been overly clear, and neither of them felt clear about any of it, except they agreed that clearly he needed another place to stay for a few months, until he could secure another place to stay for a few years, until he could secure another place to stay until death, at which time his placement would be another person's problem—not that he meant to be neglectful on that score, don't worry, he'd arrange some dark hole to crouch in.

It turned out there was a friend, *her* friend, a bachelor, who would rent Gray his extra bedroom in Brooklyn and could even set up a temporary office job for him, a low-level copyediting position at a press that specialized in brochures, alumni magazines, a line of children's books meant for waiting rooms. Gray was qualified, and since he had been saying for years that he hated his job, hated Syracuse, loved the city, it seemed to make sense. So he went on a "professional leave" from his job and took a bus to New York.

(He arrived on the day of a February parade. Banners and streamers strung up and floating. The bus rolled under them. Freezing paraders clapped and held up their batons. Gray stared out the window, dazed, handfuls of confetti falling from the sky. He got off the bus and went for a walk.)

It seemed to make sense, that is, until he arrived and discovered the apartment occupied not only by the bachelor (he had had the image of two surly men keeping to themselves, deactivating the TV before bed) but also by the bachelor's wife. Or not quite. She was almost a wife. She was nearly, approaching, had promised to be the bachelor's wife, and she took up a lot of space with her helpful storage tips and her cheery switchboard voice and her drip-drys in the bathroom.

So that's how it happened: Gray installed temporarily in a spare room with a temporary office undertaking. Gray upset about one thing (receding child) and the bachelor glad about another (impending wife).

Myers got on an airplane, an entire structure of steel coated in plastic, artificial air, stalls and slots for jamming belongings or sliding oneself into, all of it cheap and partly broken, tacked down with childproof levers.

He seated himself on the aisle. Departed along with the rest. They were all strapped down and inventoried. There was something very old in the seat next to him—man, woman, rock, he couldn't settle on what. He scanned the paper (Coney Island crime, high winds in the South, war). He got ready to arrive in a country he'd barely heard of, to a language he barely spoke (he'd had the college Spanish, yes, but he'd never expected to actually use it), to an unknown climate among other unknowns—because of course he was going to Nicaragua. Did you think he was going to go this far and give up? When he could go much, much farther, throw himself out of the country, embark on some dismal folkloric chase?

The stewards asked that everyone keep track of all the trash they carried. Not only the pieces in the overhead bins but the ones beneath the seat in front of them. The bottom ones for floatation. The ones upright and locked. The ones in the liftoff and landing.

Gray,

Maybe I'll come see this beautiful Nicaragua! In fact, I'm here. Yes, I slid down your upstate slope. I arrived in the capital just tonight. Want some company? Tell me where you are. I'm ready for a good time.

He added: *And one more thing.*

I need to ask you a question about my wife.

Gray hadn't felt comfortable living with the bachelor and the girlfriend. He tried to keep out of the way as much as possible, went for long walks, arrived at the apartment long after dinner, shut himself in his room like a teen.

And the editing job was unbearable. Not so awful, really—a mishmash of syntax, comma misplacements, general misspeak, errors of the inverbal, the lobotomized. He'd rather do anything else, anything. And he'd rather stay anyplace else as well. But Gray knew nothing about how to find a job or an apartment in the city and didn't know who to ask. He walked from one end of the island to the other, clammy with despair.

One day he found an edition of his own school's alumni magazine in the sample rack. They had a contract with his current employer. He read through it and stopped on an item about Myers. Myers had completed a layout and design certificate, had moved to Brooklyn.

Gray raised his head. Myers.

Found him in the book, phoned, got no answer. He tried each night for four nights running. He barely knew the guy but it wasn't as if he had a whole lot of other choices. He gave up finally. What would he say, anyway?

Gray suffered in the bachelor's household for four and a half months and in this time the bachelor's girlfriend became his wife and then she said it: why did she have to share her home with a man who was not only not her husband but was incapable of simple dexterous behaviors like folding and flushing? Here she was, a newlywed, and look what she had to put up with, and just as she was getting ready to do something about it, he left. Disappeared without saying goodbye, left his few items of clothing and books behind for her to bag up and trash. Rather rude. It was the last time Gray had thought about Myers until now.

Anyone watching would have noticed his name back in the course listings that fall semester and Gray back in his comp slot, and as a matter of fact, there was someone watching.

My dearest husband,

I am glad you did not drop out of the sky and into Nicaragua like a dead bird, that you chose a form of air transportation that requires supervision and accompaniment. Things are very hectic at work, to say nothing of the rest of the city. Take good care. Do not feel you have to post reports. Enjoy.

Your wife

Three arrivals and an immigration line later, Myers stepped out into the heat of the Nicaraguan night—a pandemonium of taxis, hotcake air. A hotel arm led him to a car. He rode through the night, made it up the steps. Signed the paper presented to him, allowed his belongings to be carried off.

He walked the length of the lobby, found the computer cubicles, bought a guidebook in the gift shop, sat down and went over his faults. No, he looked at something, anything other than himself. The four windows in front of him, the two desks to the side. The people coming through, walking by, going into elevators, ascending to higher floors, as if it required no effort, no sound, no remorse. A smooth lift straight up into the lighted dome. He himself rode the elevator to the mezzanine, looked over the handrail. Came back down.

He would not have to go far to see the Nicaraguan wonders around him, his guidebook informed him. There was a *live, smoking volcano* right on the outskirts of town that anyone could visit and witness, no special permits necessary and no volcanic equipment either because it wasn't going to explode in anyone's face and lots of people lived all around it and walked over it every day and planted their corn on it and they didn't have to wear any special hats or protective goggles. And on top of having a *live, smoking volcano*, they had earthquakes too, and everybody had to hold on to their hats or they could topple over like plastic army men and you didn't see them complaining. To witness this special volcanic event all one had to do was take a bus or a taxi, ride up the volcanic slant, observe the billows of smoke that rise from the pit of the earth, have one's moment of fear or awe or existential crisis in the face of this bit of torn-up planet, then get back in the transport and return to the hotel. This is a fine adventure and many others are available as well but one has to choose, one always must.

And a few blocks from where his feet now rested was Nicaragua's very own indoor, climate-controlled shopping mall, built in the happy tradition of Victor Gruen, a confirmation of Nicaragua's social and aesthetic alignment with the modern. The guidebook had an impressive list of items Myers could purchase and take back to his country, and had a photograph of the escalator he could ride and of the food court he'd reach at the top. He could see it for himself if he followed the little map over the sidewalks and through the labyrinth of traffic. Who knew what awaited him on the other side of the street if he'd only step across? And there's no sense in acting like a snob about it, acting like you're going to come all the way here and not want to shop, no sense in that, because everyone knows that everyone wants to shop no matter where you're from or who you are, everyone wants to, everyone. What else did you come all the way here for, if not to seize and take back what you also have at home?

Myers,

Regional manager here. I don't believe we've come to a good understanding about the phone call that took place between us. I believe something went wrong between my voice and your ears, between your mouth and my phone, between my words and your deeds, between the wires, Myers, between one hotel and another, between one thought and the next. I'm talking about you. Your thoughts, your feet. They did not, I notice, bring you and your laptop back here. You've got until tomorrow. I'm shoving your desk over a cliff in the morning. I'll watch it smash on the rocks below.

The country also featured any number of "volunteers" at any given time. These volunteers, not unlike Santa's elves, hailed from Myers's very own country as well as from helpful guilt-ridden European ones, such as Germany. He could observe these volunteers in a wild-habitat location and witness their good works for himself. The country was stuffed with these people, frankly, so much so that sometimes they couldn't quite fit and had to be tied together with bamboo rope and sent home on a raft. But this year the country had just the right amount of volunteers and you could glimpse them from several vantage points, taking a break from their labors of latrine digging and stair building or from making their solemn advisements in regards to matters of business, religion, childcare, gardening, and diplomacy. The Nicaraguans are careful with them. They don't burn the volunteers by leaving them out too long in the sun or drown them by throwing them into the sea. They don't place them under a mango tree, because a piece of fruit could fall on their heads and knock them over. They don't lock the volunteers out in the rain or accidentally run them over with their trucks. They feed them every day and encourage them to propagate among themselves. The Nicaraguans don't say things like, What do you think, that we can't perfectly well dig our own toilets? Get out of the way, would you? Go build your stairs over there where no one will trip on them, for Pete's sake. They never say that. Because it's not easy out there for the volunteers with only their little sewing machines and toy shovels to work with. Besides, it's nice to have them around. It's a lot better than getting exploded by hundred-pound bombs. It's a lot better than getting smeared into vapors in the air.

Myers, you old crater-head,

Glad you decided to come. Nicaragua is the most beautiful place in the world. So you're married, old man. I didn't know. Congratulations, I say! Bring her over, I'd love to meet her. I don't know what I can answer for you. I haven't had much luck in the on-the-hook myself—I'm a divorcé with a

leftover shoot, as you might have read in the alumni notes. But I'll advise as best I can. My mind is an enormous unscrolled newsreel. Bring some aspirin. I have a splitting headache.
    Gray

Myers walked the lobby end to end. Two doormen stationed for night duty stared impassively after him. He passed them over and over. Didn't know he was married... Oh, he had a splitting ache for the guy, all right. He'd make a watermark on the pavement with Gray's brain. He wondered what the laws here were.

The world teemed out there, unmoored. He plugged letters into the screen, felt less every moment, felt nothing, felt dull. The gift shop closed. Behind the glass sat the T-shirt and postcard set-ups, the beach equipment, scuba stuff, drown book, sand machine. He wandered down another hall. Found the restaurant. Empty, dim. Coat check in its cubbyhole. Tablecloths covering their four edges. The window had a view of the city. The hotel, perched on its rock like a rat, its head bobbing over the whatnot—the waterline of town, the sunk sun. A pattern of antennae on rooftops, pale lines of sky. Inside was orderly, milk-clean, as if implying that the mind could be like that, as if that drastic mess in the brain could be straightened. You could go inside and smooth everything over like a fresh roller of paint over dirty walls, hide the filth underneath, cover it over, shove it down in there, hard.

Sure, I'll come. Where are you, Gray?

Above him, down hallways, doors shut. Guests performed their weary nightly series of floss, undress, sex. Clocks rocked to a stop for the dark hours. The doormen held their deadpan positions.

Myers believed in nothing and nobody, but somebody had an eye on him, must have, or else he would have paced all night. Somebody corralled him like a little mouse in, yes, a maze, lifting this wall, blocking that entrance, drawing a line down a corridor, an arrow for him to scurry over, a pellet at the foot of the door. And the night finally ended with him sitting down on the bed, at the edge of it, wedged into this country (how'd he get himself into this?), in the one room Gray obviously wasn't (at least he was in the right country now), eyes closing, leaning back, his thoughts going along the edges, along the windowsill, the shower-stall ledge, along the night table, the edge of light and the space on the other side of the door, through it, over it, to the woman he'd left behind.

Chapter Six

It took a month for Myers to see that she was following someone else.

At first he noticed nothing but her. Her figure on the street filled his mind. He saw no one in front of her. Then he did. Once, twice. The same shuffle, the slouch in the crowd. At last it was plain: *she was following a man.*

Long jacket, briefcase in hand, hat. A man. A year or two younger than Myers. A little thinner, an inch shorter. Not so unlike Myers. He hiked along. People collected on the sidewalks. He drew into them and emerged without any special flair. He raised a hand to adjust the forward tilt of his hat in the same way Myers might.

That's what she was doing. She watched from the corner or she sat on a bar stool a few feet away. She waited for the man to come out of shops. She followed him down stairs to the subway. In rain, she stepped his paintbrush line, slickered by Myers who had berated her into wearing rain gear that morning, knowing she'd be out in a storm following some goddamn man around.

And this: *she did not know him*. Or rather, he did not know her. He never bothered to look her way, nod or smile, never worked his way to her table to say hello, never held open the door if she was behind him. Now and then he pivoted and she swerved into his view. He did not take her in. His eyes went over her, unstirred, buzzless. She did not heap up his heart in any way at all.

The three of them were walking along like a shifty Simon Says. Myers tracking his wife tracking a stranger. The stranger was pulling them along like a string toy.

What the hell did she think she was doing following some guy all over creation? And if Myers was expected to believe there was anything innocent in it—well, did she think he was a complete and utter fool?

At night Myers lay next to her. He dreamed that she was dreaming of the man. He dreamed that he, Myers, was absent and that man was here—and that man was lying here dreaming of his wife.

If anyone thought Myers was going to give away his position now, they had another thing coming.

Best-case scenario: The guy had committed a crime she had witnessed. Another guy had committed a crime and this man was the victim. She needed to tell him something. Someone paid her to follow him, it was a job she made money at and invested in secret. There were other reasons—political, philosophical, messianic. She expected terrible or wonderful events to stem from him. She had gone mad.

Next, this: *he* knew the man. Or thought he did. The man was familiarish. He got a quick look in a men's room. Then a long stare from the side. Where had Myers seen that face?

A procession of images passed behind his eyes.

The name didn't come at first, just the outline of his head against a collegiate backdrop. Then the shoulders, the form of him, a figure propped up at the bus stop years ago, of him bent over his tray in the dorm café. Myers lay the one over the other, stood them beside the man now receding down the street while Myers found himself stunned into a standstill.

Illumination. Gold came up in the pan.

The name was Gray.

They argued. It was her birthday and he stupidly said he loved her, handed the words over along with a gift, stupid because he didn't feel like he did that day but he said it, he loved her, and she said, I don't even know what that is. He said, That's a nice comment to make to your husband, and she said, fine, she was just saying what was on her mind. If he wanted, she could keep what was on her mind where it was.

Odd thing to have on her mind, he said, considering she had heard him say it for almost two years running, not to mention on their very wedding night.

They were in the bedroom when this happened. Not in the bed but by the closet door. She was half-dressed and dressing further, getting ready to meet her friend Anita for a birthday dinner. He was half-undressed because he was staying home, had stayed home from work (had been missing too much) because he had come down with the flu (who wouldn't, zigzagging around in the rain like an umbrella?) and was on his way to bed. He knew she'd ditch her friend and follow that man by herself.

She doesn't know what that is, he mumbled. There are many things that he is that he doesn't know what are.

You damn well used to know the word before, he said.

What word?

Love. As in, I love you.

I didn't say I didn't know the word, she said. I said I didn't know what you meant when you said it.

Next, this: *she* didn't know his name. Myers tried to be cute, said Gray's name aloud, called him a client, inserted him into news stories, but she looked as bored as ever, as sunk into her own cesspit, and it was obvious— she'd never heard of him. Which why should that surprise him? Why else follow someone through sleet and sun, around the ironwork of this city, other than because you don't know who he is?

For Christ's sake. Jesus.

So she lied and sneaked with a regularity matched only by the rising sun and anybody within a few feet of her (Myers) was just going to have to live with it, buddy, and he certainly was.

What do you mean what did he mean? He didn't know what he meant. I love you. He said it like he always does.

Married people say that all the time, he said.

It's a vulgar phrase, she said. It means nothing. Why not simply say what you mean?

He wasn't the only vulgar one. Might he remind her that she herself had said it many, many times herself?

The man Gray, whom his wife followed, sat alone in restaurants near other men who looked more or less like him, youngish, early thirties, also alone. No one seemed terrified of him or angry or alarmed. No one seemed to think that guy better get out of there or that he was some sort of sexual deviant. No one changed tables or moved farther down the bar at his approach. He wasn't peculiar. He was normal-sized, normal-voiced, normal, not eccentric. Myers's wife was normal-sized and normal-faced as well. And Myers too, normal. You never saw so many normal people sitting around calmly looking and not looking at each other.

They walked up broad streets, then narrow ones, fire escapes hanging overhead, water dripping from windows. And they walked by the opera house and the symphony and other cultural spots, museums of various sizes, some small enough to fit in a storefront window, some that took a block to approach and another to leave behind, a band of yammering tourists stamping outside. Inside—once Gray tramped them through some large art edifice—were the regulation objects, bottles and pictures, shipped in and stood up at intervals, identifying haiku on a tag below each one, telling what each one was in desponding abstraction. They wove through rooms, Myers a room or two behind. He stifled his own breathing, which had a distinguishable jagged lag due to a childhood accident. He thought she might recognize the sound and go back. It felt like they were walking through the maze of their own graves at that point.

If she no longer said it, that implied she was saying she didn't.

She never said she was saying that. She never said she didn't love him anymore.

Then what was she saying?

She didn't know, she just didn't know, and could they go one day, one *hour*, without an extravagant fight?

That, then her, walking out the door.

After that he didn't say it anymore and neither did she. Its absence entered and chilled him.

He had a very penetrating stride, this guy. The most varied step Myers had ever seen, as if he suspected there were people trailing him and he wasn't going to make it easy on anybody. The man continuously changed his pace, sped up, paused, raised an arm to his hat, examined the lines of newspaper machines or looked into a store window, then abruptly broke into an even step. Who knew just what this was about. He'd begin down a long street, then he'd stop, reverse himself as if he'd just remembered some smashed sandwich on his desk and meant to go back and retrieve it. This set off a whole chain of reactions down the street with her hurrying out of the line of vision and Myers as well. Then just as suddenly the guy would change his mind and go back the other way.

In some neighborhoods they passed numerous burned-out shops. Once Myers counted a dozen little stores blackened with soot, a wall or two caved in, yellow police tape ribboned around the front. These places were sort of scattered around, trolling out to the north. And there were also the hospitals that cropped up at corners and then went on for whole blocks, growing out of the ground, even the signage and sidewalks affected, so that the area transformed into a special medical sub-city, separate from the one a stoplight or two back.

The man left work between 5:25 and 6:10 and to get himself awake he would take a brisk walk. Myers and his wife would follow along. He'd go just about anywhere—by either river, under overpasses, it didn't matter. He could go on for hours that way.

One night he was walking and he was going on and on, through the turns and sway of the vast park (the one dark blot in the middle of the city, yes, let's have a stroll there by all means, why not, sure, his wife alone-ish, unprotected), and they went on and on and it got probably to be about eleven at night, and Myers fell asleep. As a matter of fact, before he fell asleep he thought to himself: My God, I'm going to fall asleep, and he did. He just kept going along, dozing, he must have, because the next thing he knew, he crashed into a park map-board and woke up. He didn't know how long he'd been walking or where he was or how long he'd been asleep, but his wife was gone and Gray was gone. Somehow the man had led her out of there and somehow safely home.

The ground froze. It chipped under their shoes. Gray remained in the Battery area, moving in swift circles until the streets emptied and the place took on an industrial sheen. Dark shapes patched the sky. The street shone like a river. The posters were coming off the walls in paper flakes. Gray walked ahead. Only her shoes made sound—a light squeak now and then, almost nothing. She paused as if listening. Had she heard Myers? She looked like a struck match, light hair blowing, body trembling. She did not turn. No one saw anyone who wasn't supposed to. Myers held up a finger and blotted her out.

Then they all went on.

They had another fight. This time about the storage room. No, it was the storage-room lock, which she couldn't put on, which any human being in this pulsing metro area could manage to fasten except his wife. The simplest gadget in existence. Oh and here came another spiel from her unsimple husband, another lecture that she was going to have to get around or on top of, push in its stop.

Gray himself, when Myers managed a glance, always had the same startled look on his face, as if he'd just received an insult. And he seemed not to know how to stop once set in motion, apart from the pauses and the demented jerks.

If you think about it, everyone is behind someone and in front of someone. The nature of the sphere, right? No one gets left at the end or is forced to take the lead, and in this way you might say the shape of the earth is democratic. There are hesitations, of course. There are lines going in ways that you wouldn't imagine. People are passed up or passed over. The tempo is irregular and messy. If you thought about the entirety of it, the legs, the back and forth, it's a fiasco, an anarchy of steps. It's impossible. And there's no way to tidy it or make it in any way manageable, not in one's imagination or anywhere else.

After all, it was exhausting enough—the job, the wife, the commute, the wandering after her until all hours of the night. Just getting food into one's body was a chore. It was absurd, how could anyone do what they did and have to come home and talk about anything other than lights or locks? But was he going to confront her before he knew what she was up to so she could come up with some outrageous lie and then he'd never find out the truth? It all seemed like a nightmare in any case, and he wasn't entirely certain he wouldn't wake up soon.

It wasn't about the arguing, of course, but one of them seemed to decide to pretend it was about the arguing and the other without saying so agreed and then there was no going back, it fixed between them: None of this would be happening if we didn't argue so much. This is how it started to add up, bit by bit.

They fought. The tea. One of them didn't want it but the other had made it anyway and the result was two cups when there should have been only one. The one who didn't want it had said so, but too softly, and the other hadn't heard.

The one who didn't want it always speaks too softly.

The one who made it never hears.

The one who didn't want it never knows what to want and what not to.

The one who made it always wants too much.

And this was like other things in their love. It was like sex in their love. Or lack of. (Ahem?) Or at least less of. It was like cooperation in their love. It was like friendship in their love. And/or it revealed their love, an aspect of it they had not previously identified, had not yet protested.

It was a terrible thing what had happened with the tea.

It was an act committed in duty but resulting in alienation. No, it was a passive act resulting in aggression. No, it was a demonstration, a lesson, a portent.

She hadn't gone hobbling off after complete strangers when they met, of course, but it had to have been somewhat inside her all along. A thing like that doesn't grow out of nothing, without divine intervention, without a seed in the soil, without a small star, so small no one could see it, that one day explodes.

No, it was there but no one could see it and somehow it had grown. He himself must have watered it or blown it up with air or thrown more wood on it or tacked more pieces to it because how could this wife have come from that one without her husband's help?

No, he had no intention at all of revealing what he knew.

Where have you been? was the most he'd give away.
    I didn't know I had a curfew, she said.
    I called you at work.
    I didn't know I was in lockdown.
    They said you'd left.
    Nobody told me about the martial law.

He left off following her to follow other women. He could be unfaithful in the same way she was, easily. The women went down sidewalks, through subways, out into crisp air. They clipped up the block, over fall leaves, to their brownstones. So what was he now, a stalker? He went home.

He trailed Gray when she didn't. He called home and made excuses, called work and made excuses. Now the guy was being watched by both of them. And he was a wanderer, this Gray. He got around. But Myers discovered nothing. Only routines, broken or kept. Split roads, silence amid street noise. Grim.

What I do is my business, she said.
    Apparently.

I am not your employee.

That's some luck. I'd fire you.

I am not your dog.

You don't seem like anything these days. You seem like a vacant stare.

Do you think I don't know that? she said. Do you think I don't see myself?

The tea fight, and then had come the walkouts. She yelled something and walked out the back door and stood outside on the landing. He walked out the front door and stood under the trees. Then he walked around the building and looked up at her looking up. And then she looked down and saw him and went back inside. He walked around the front and went back in too. He called to her, said something in a new voice, something about the tea, a thing he hoped would be conciliatory and that he hoped would make her say something conciliatory back. Instead she said her own new thing about the tea, or the dishes really, in general, how they were never clean unless she did them, and then she started crying and he got up and tried to comfort her. Leave me *alone*! she said and moved her shoulder around, and he went into the bathroom and when she called to him he locked the door, which he knows she hates. Then she took his newspaper out of his briefcase, which she knows he hates, and she looked up apartments for rent because she was throwing him out and he knew she was doing this because she called it to him through the bathroom door. Then she looked at airfares in the travel section because she was sending him away and he knew this because she called it to him through the bathroom door too. Then she looked at the personals, which she knows he hates, read aloud who might be better for her than him and he knew she was doing it because she called this to him too through the bathroom door. Then she just sat there sniffling and taking apart the newspaper because she knows he hates that, and she called that to him too. I'm leaving you, she said, and I'm taking the paper with me. Blow a kiss goodbye. I'm going out the window, she said. Throwing myself out and I'm throwing your paper out first. I'm taking the window with me. I'm taking the door. Better come out, she said. Soon there'll be nothing left but you.

Chapter Seven

CLAIRE

Last week the phone rang. This is how I wound up on the train.

We have a box here in Chicago, said the woman on the phone. We thought you might like to know.

It was early. I was half-asleep in my bathrobe, propped up in a chair.

Thank you for the update, I said. Maybe next time you could take out an announcement in the *Times*.

It's a box with your mother's papers in it—your mother, the TV star?

If this is blackmail, you go ahead and show those to anyone you want.

This is not blackmail.

Pawn shop? Mob?

Librarian. Your father sold these to us on condition that they stay sealed until now.

What's so special about now? I said. I looked at the clock.

Your father's been dead ten years today.

He wasn't my father.

Whoever he was, the box is here and on top is a card with your name on it. As of today these papers are a matter of public record to anyone with a fine-free card. But you get first look, if you care to, which you might, considering.

Considering what?

Don't ask me. It's your family.

At first I wasn't going to go. I had a lot to do myself. I don't know why he had to sell them to a place way out west.

Ha. I was going. Of course I was going. My mother's papers? You bet I was going. I never got to ask the woman a single question. And the man who raised me just made his broadcast and died.

At first I wasn't going to go because the truth was I had no money, or the truth was I was going to go when I had the money—it always comes along sometime. No, the truth was I had no money but clearly now I needed some money because I had to find out what was in that box. I needed money now.

I was up at this hour because I didn't want to be in bed. There was a stranger in there who I hoped would wake up soon and leave.

Hey, wake up, I called. I went over to him. You have to get up now.

He opened his eyes. I dreamed the phone was ringing, he said.

It was just a dream, I said.

He sat up, pulled on his shirt.

Your dog wants to be let in, he said. Don't you hear that?

I don't have a dog, I said.

I fastened a hairpin in my hair.

Do you have any cash? I said.

He blinked at me.

It's for my mother.

So I took the subway to the train station and got on the train. I'd only been seated a few minutes before the man sat down next to me, the one with the head. He had just the single odd feature, like a trick with mirrors or papîer-mâché. Or perhaps as if he had been lying down for a long time with a small weight pressing into the side of his head, and each day a smaller weight was put on top of the one that was there, and another and another. At first the weight would have been nothing. A fly to swat. Tax. Almost not there. But one day it wasn't nothing anymore —the accumulation, the duration pushed it (inward) to subtle, devastating proportions. It's all just math.

Later, after he'd left his seat and I saw him out on the platform, I realized who he resembled. An image of the man who raised me came into my mind: We were playing nuclear war together and making sounds of sirens. We were laughing. I'd drawn on the mirror with soap a bomb going into the ocean. Mayday! he was saying. Man down!

Chapter Eight

In the capital Myers woke. Cool dim room. A sinking dream of water. An inkling, a sensation almost of pleasure: he'd find Gray today. He placed his feet on the carpet. The exterior hung in the window. A scroll of low houses unwound on a hill. A card on the nightstand apprised him: *We're proud to serve you!*

Somehow the next thing that happened was that Myers lost his job.

There was no ceremony to it. He got into his clothes, made it down to the business center, opened his browser, saw the message, sat back in his chair. He didn't open the email, didn't have to. What else could Human Resources want with him? Besides, the subject line gave it away. Really, it was hard to believe it could be official, coming in this way, as an early lifeless streak of light.

Outside, the Nicaraguan sun was getting around, blinking on the screen.

He put off opening the email, pushed the moment ahead of him because at this moment he was just a man sitting in an office chair. Yes, once he read it he would still be a man sitting in an office chair, but that sitting man would be different, so it would look different, though it would look exactly the same. He wanted to look like he did, a man in this chair with that job, rather than one without it, a little longer. He closed his eyes.

He tried to imagine a black line growing out in both directions. He tried to imagine a quiet sea.

He had no message from Gray.

My dearest wife, he typed.

It is beautiful here despite the heat and there is quite a bit of that. It seems to be the main feature. They have certainly got a handle on that end of it, on keeping it turned up high, on not letting anybody get cold.

The hotel is. The food is. The sights are. The language.

Wish you

Wish for you

He stopped. Deleted.

It seemed to him that he'd had in his life very few surprises in the category of employment. He'd had only long slow failings, was defeated in increments, scheduled disappointments.

Tourist shrubs lined the walk. In the lobby, giant dry leaves drooped from the palms. A woman was cleaning the plastic-upholstered interior.

Where the hell could Gray be? This hotel seemed practically empty.

My dearest wife, he began again, with a slight shake in his hand.

It is beautiful here, somewhat like Florida but shaped differently, more squat than long. Splotchlike. Imagine ink spill. Water spot. Broke yolk. I did have fine eggs for breakfast.

Having a good. Thinking of. Sending you. Farewell from. Warm wish. Weather.

Deleted.

Well, he had the hotel home page to look at (¡*Nica Linda!*), featuring the less farfetched of the tourist destinations: Granada, a mere sixty kilometers from the capital, more tourists per capita than any town in the Americas, the most beautiful…

There was a lot to like about the job. There was the pay, the location, the copy machine (which actually worked), his office, its window, client dinners, bonuses, the nightly janitorial wastebasket service. There was the regional manager and the one over him, both reasonably reasonable people, not imbecilic dummies. The lack of outdated technology—a relief after the slide-rule days of his last job, of setting black-and-white photos of schoolrooms into templates three years old. There was being in downtown proper, not all the way over, almost shoved off the island. There was the lack of undignified, leg-numbing, IQ-depleting training sessions. The lack of humiliating pay. The lack of humiliations of many sorts.

Outside, the sky didn't even look like sky, it was almost not there behind the smog haze, the antennae and rebar. It was just the filler between crowded objects.

At last he opened the email. It was a shot to the brain that did not stagger him but sunk in deeply and stayed.

From: HR
Subject: Termination of Employment
   This is to inform you that your employment has been terminated with cause *effective immediately. Given that your termination is with cause, there is no requirement for our company to give you either notice or termination pay.*

Company property in your possession must be returned within forty-eight hours or legal proceedings will begin. A registered letter has been sent to the home address listed in your human resources file. Please be in receipt of it. Personals to follow to same.

No way was Gray around here. Myers was the only tourist in sight. He stood, left the business room, left the lobby, packed, left. Time to find this jackass.

The capital: boxes collected in fields. Very hot out there, no kidding around. The heat was like a religion. It was like a throat closing shut. Myers took a taxi through a racket of streets and a few twirls of barbed wire. He'd get to the main tourist artery. When he heard from Gray he'd be right there, ready. He didn't see Gray outside on the sidewalks, but he saw many others, bricklayers or statesmen or so on. And what was that walking bird-creature—a rooster? Other animalia: what appeared to be cow. Next to it, a smaller sprightlier version, possibly goat. He'd only worked at the place for four months. He was ineligible for unemployment. Suppose he'd have to live on the beach like a penguin now. Suppose he'd have to mime in the park. He arrived at the bus station.

CLAIRE

I arrived in Chicago and got off the train. There were a lot of us here, each in our own mortal slipcase. I walked along the freezing cement. I wove through the buildings and came out onto a huge lake and suddenly I remembered the word "horizontal." Where I live I never see expanse like this. The library was sixty blocks south of downtown, long ones, and I walked them all, the city on my right, a dog padding behind me. I could hear a few birds softly squeak.

I got to the library. The building was the color and material of a tombstone. The librarian inspected me.

I need to ask you some security questions, she said, reading from a card. Mother's birthplace, maiden name, age at time of death, college mascot.

She didn't go to college, I said.

The elevator ding sounded behind me. The librarian pulled out a folder.

Where's the box? I said. This is it? This is what we call a folder, not a box.

She shrugged.

I opened the folder. Among the receipts, the hairdo instructions, the contracts, I found a letter addressed to me.

Myers boarded a bus. It was more than full and kept filling. It was as bad as the bus where he was from. Four people squeezed into a seat for two and more kept getting on. The windows could apparently be opened only by trained engineers. Telephone poles linked and receded. The heat was a beak on the skin. But it was fine. He'd find Gray and tangle him into the hotel bedsprings.

The man in the next seat knew a little English. How long are you here? he wanted to know.

How long am I where? Myers said.

He'd had a single bad week, plus maybe a few mediocre months. He'd had a moment of crisis, of transformation, perhaps for his better, had counted on the understanding of his superiors. Instead of support he got sand in the eyes, he got blood in the mouth, fish bones in the throat, he got pushed off the platform before he'd had his say.

This was the way of treating him.

He rode out of Managua.

CLAIRE

My dearest Claire, my mother wrote. *Your real father is Mexican. I met him on a water shoot I did in Cancún. He is a respectable man with a respectable job. Nothing strange there. He trains dolphins—as most people would, given the time and inclination. He is not much different from your stepfather, the man who is raising you as his own. On a practical level, they're nearly interchangeable. You could switch their clothes, their occupations, countries of origin, and you might confuse them.*

I don't know if it will help you to know this. I thought I should tell you. I hope you'll be an adult about this. Your stepfather, by the way, didn't even feel it.

There it is, folks. My mother pens from the grave. She'd signed her name the way she did autographs. I put the envelope back in the folder. Then I saw there was a picture in there. A photo.

A man, standing poolside with hoop.

I imagined them both, both my fathers, side by side, as if they were cutouts printed on a piece of cardboard that you could snip, one or the other. They looked nothing alike.

At the other end of the counter the librarian had a phone in her hand.

I put the photo into my bag.

Hey, the librarian shouted. Hey! She was rushing over.

I left the folder on the counter. I pushed the door and went back out to the street.

Chapter Nine

So on the third day of his vacation and the first of his unemployment, Myers stepped off the bus in the tourist hot spot Granada, which his guidebook described as "colonial," an adjective which refers to the ornamental aspects of one group coming in and removing another by frog-march or slaughter or other means of diplomacy. The town was cobbled, shingled, whitewashed. He'd overturn every cobblestone in the country if he had to. He checked in to a hotel.

At reception, a young American couple leaned over and introduced themselves as Christians. Not only that, they'd just arrived.

So what? What did Myers care?

And what did the guy beside him care either? There was a guy beside him who said he'd had enough of Nicaragua and if *he'd* just arrived, he'd leave.

Now look, said the Christians, this is a perfectly nice town. Who wants to go for a walk?

Myers wasn't interested in any Christian walk.

Neither was the other guy.

No, no, the Christians said. We're non-evangelical. A secular walk.

Myers didn't know what was so non-evangelical about saying you're Christians in the first sentence of meeting someone.

Forget the Christian part, they said. That was just a little extra side thing. And forget the walk. If you don't want to go, fine. Stay here in your hotel room and look at the towel rack. What do we care.

Myers wasn't saying he didn't want to go but can a guy put his crap down and check his email first? Jesus.

The other guy wasn't going. He knew what it looked like outdoors.

The other guy, who had been robbed twice in Managua by kids no taller than ducks.

Who rode here on a bus that sounded like a circus.

Who hadn't seen a single taxi with seatbelts that work.

Who couldn't believe the piles of trash. Even in the countryside, where there was nothing, there was another pile of trash. This was the first place he'd been that was sort of clean.

The other guy, who (it occurred to Myers) actually looked Nicaraguan, who had to be Nicaraguan.

The other guy wasn't going anywhere. He was staying inside.

Myers had no new messages.

The outdoors turned out to consist of a few locals, some bleached buildings, and many many saddish slowish herdish Americans arranged in clusters (Myers looked them over: none of them were Gray) and here and there a fully formed tour team with a loud guide. Daypacks, cameras, water bottles, flip-flops all around.

It was decided (the Christians decided) that the best way to view the sights was to follow the lines drawn in the guidebook, lines that created mazes and intersected with points of interest. The excursionist could move from spot to spot in a space/time-efficient manner. Used correctly, the system worked somewhat like a conveyor belt, or a merry-go-round, or like interstellar rotations charted from the ground.

Myers wiped at sweat with his handkerchief, nodded at the large-leaf trees, the stone benches. Somewhere nearby a church bell was going off.

Charming, he said politely. Very nice.

Certainly damn well worth losing his job over. He glanced around for Gray. Indeed.

The town lies at the edge of a beautiful saltwater lake, a Christian said. He was reading from the same guidebook Myers had, the same one everyone had, with the exception of a few Europeans walking by who had one with a title that contained the word "foot." The Christian was saying something about sawtooth sharks in that lake. Something about bones on the beach, about four hundred islands, they all fit in the lake, plus room for water and boats.

It says there are many trees and food stalls. Also civic buildings, the Christian read. He lowered the book. Lovely! he said.

They walked over to the cathedral and stood on the steps outside. They were reading about all the people who had attacked the town and burned it to the ground—first the pirates, then the French, then the British, then one lone American on a horse, and more could be on the way.

Myers might have put off his trip a few days. He'd waited two years already. He could have finished up a few things at the office and caught up with Gray next week. That element of vacation he had failed in. Above him the cathedral looked like the slate of white in his brain, and below him the steps seemed as though they continued on down into the earth.

He and the Christians turned and went in.

The usual gowned saints. Robed saints. Saints raising objects. Saints patting the heads of saint-sheep.

He might have waited the week, done his damnedest as far as work went, then asked for an early half-month. He could have waited the week but had chosen not to. It was dark—Gray could be in here and Myers wouldn't even see him.

But would Gray be in a cathedral?

Come on, said Myers. Let's go.

They came back out and walked on.

This was not the most beautiful place in the world, whatever Gray had to say about it. They walked by something else that looked like something else he saw at home—house, car, billboard, shop—only a little less so, looking a little less like a house at home than usual, in regard to materials, as far as the sides of the house, and what held them down, and as far as the roof, the rounded tiles that covered the top.

And he heard sounds like any sound he knew anywhere—cicadas, rock music, honks—only a little more so, since his ears were involved in listening, not in shutting out. He didn't see the big deal, in any case. Other country, piece of earth, a gathering of people unknown to Myers, lonely land, not so unlike his own, hotter, better lit, a different group of strangers on the streets. The sun was a knot in the sky. Myers strolling along.

Before the earthquake and all that came after, he followed the Christians to the famous museum of pre-Columbian art. Now how do you like that, clay animals and such right there in a case for everyone to see, a bric-a-brac reminder. That's history for you. That's the sort of thing you don't get in a book. You have to be on the beat to see something like that. Imagine living right here and seeing this any time you want. Imagine what that would do to a person. The quiet pride that would grow in the heart. Why, one of the Christians might snap a picture of that. There's the thing to do. Take it home. He might stand here a while. Reflect.

The other Christian might step outside, light a cigarette.

Should you be doing that? Myers said. Isn't your body your temple?

Fuck off, she said.

Should you be talking like that? Isn't your mouth your temple?

One of the Christians might wander into the museum courtyard and stare sadly at a monkey on a chain who lay panting on a square of cement.

Myers found him. What's the matter with your girlfriend?

She wanted to go to El Salvador, where the real martyrs are. She wanted hardship. I told her being a Christian is hard enough.

Myers scoffed. Come off it. What's so hard about it?

Faith is hard.

What's hard? All you have to do is think something.

It's a lot harder than staying alive, which is all *you* have to do.

True, but that's because what you have to think is so weird. Of course it's hard to believe a thing like that.

This isn't a Christian walk, remember? said the Christian.

Funny, the first place we went was a church.

Even if he wanted to, he couldn't search all the towns. Look at this map. The towns dotted the page in casual disorder. And he wasn't going to be able to inspect every tourist. There were hundreds of them, limping around with their sissy bottles of water, Myers among them, one of them. The Nicaraguans were all right, not waving the tourists away like stray dogs or chasing them off with sticks. Everybody seemed to get on fairly well. But the whole experience was inconvenient for one thing, lots of getting up and sitting down, lots of staring at the pages of the guidebook while trying to walk without bumping into anything and pitching over. And the entire affair was too hot, as if a madman had come along and heated the place up—really outrageous—and everyone walking around as if it were normal, as if the heat were the least interesting outrageous experience of the day.

So the plan was: Find Gray, go home, apply for employment, continue to function. In that order.

So far it had been more or less a successful day for the majority of U.S. citizens present. No one had gotten hurt or fallen down. No one had lost their money or been left behind. There had been no bizarre conversations or accusations. No one tried to block a tourist's path and said the tourist looked suspect. No tourist spoke beyond the required niceties and strained efforts to make themselves understood. All was in order. Only Myers was not getting his money's worth. But he still had nine more vacation days left on his plane ticket, nine more days to disjoint this country and shake out the man.

They made a right. Continued down another stretch. Fine business! a Christian said approvingly. Their sewer committee seems to be in friendly relations with each other, which is more than I can say for our hometown.

The other Christian did something with her eyes.

Hey, said the first Christian. Why do you have to do that?

Do what?

He turned to Myers. Did you see what she did?

Um, Myers said. I'm going to check my email. He walked away down the street, leaving them standing at odd angles from each other behind him.

He ducked into an Internet café, sat down, and clicked Retrieve.

Now, he had read all the earthquake advisory materials he had come into contact with in the guidebook, on the cathedral wall, in the *¡Vamos, Nica!* brochure in his room—information about collapsing walls, flying glass, fore- and aftershocks, doorways, falling objects, utility wires, exterior structures, ground movement. Don't panic. Stay in bed. Put a pillow over your head. Go to your Department Evacuation Assembly Point. Stay as safe as possible. But there was hardly time to take private measures. When the earthquake came, Myers found himself on the floor of the Internet facility.

Before falling out of his chair, he checked his email, snipped three spams from the stem, and then saw it: Gray had responded at last.

Got your note, Myers. Where the hell is Granada? Seems to me that's in Spain Here's a hard rock for you—right between the blades. The head is a difficult object, Myers. I've been giving it some thought. The worst is when you can't get the thing off, though it looks like you yourself may have tried a time or two...

The mention of the head didn't make much sense. He had never told Gray about his childhood accident.

...Glad to hear you're joining me, Myers. Once you're here the true vacation begins: two college buddies hit the sights, eat foods that seem strange to them, have moments they'll always remember, buy trinkets—I have seen exactly zero in the trinkets regard, by the way. Where are the trinkets? The painted bowls, the woven shoes, the bird whistle?...

At that moment the Granada earthquake hit, but compared to Gray's email, it seemed pretty minor. The earth could crack in half for all Myers cared. It would barely race the bland rhythm of his heart. Gray's email was the real business going on. But it was so odd and so far from describing the experience Myers was having that it made him wonder if there'd been a mistake, if Myers had confused the thing, ended up in the wrong country, on the wrong continent, following the wrong man, separated from the right one by time and ocean, if there were two Nicaraguas.

...Oh, we'll have enough to do, Myers. We'll dust off the old Esperanto dictionary. Dig out the grammar and tapes, do our part for world unification. Let's spend an evening at the local food bank, hang out the blocks of cheese, stir up the spaghetti. By God, I talked about solutions back in the day. Brick in the toilet, union strike, Marshall Plan. The world's not going to end but it sure is going to slow down, my friend.

You might hurry a bit. I need you just now. I asked my ex to send my little girl, but the poor thing's barely into panties. I don't think she'd be much use in any case...

A little earthquake. Not as small as a tremor but nothing to get all clobbered over. A sideshow earthquake. The five-and-ten kind. Flea fair.

The first he knew he was on the floor. Not the first. The first he knew the desk had wheels because it was moving. This desk has wheels, he thought, because it is moving, but he could see very well that it had no wheels because he was looking at its feet. Then he was on the floor with a heavy thing on top of him. No, first the wheels when there were none, then the sound (what he would later recall as the earthquake sound, no other sound like it in the world, he would say to whoever was listening, and no one would be), then the floor with a cement block crushing one side of him. So wheels, then sound, then him falling over, because the ground was buckling. The ground shoved him up in his chair and then over. So wheels, sound, ground, the crack of his own bone. End to end it couldn't have been more than twenty seconds.

...Get over here, Myers. Do you understand? Sway this way. Approach. Fleet

leg. Meet me on Corn Island. The most beautiful island in the world. I'll see
you at the hotel.

    Gray

It was not the only time he'd felt the ground move. There was the time he
and his wife went to the ocean—who says they'd never taken a vacation?
They'd had a terrific time. They went floating on a raft, drifting, the
ocean belly below them. Behind them the land looked like ash. But after
a few hours this way the sky darkened and the raft turned in circles and
they had a small struggle making it back. He swore that it was the earth
bucking them out farther. No, she had said. The world spinning around
the way it does, she said, of course the soup is going to stir.

His eyes opened and he blinked through the grit. He went over it again,
did not understand. Gray needed him? He raised his head slightly. His
arm was bent the wrong way under the cement partition. Corn Island?
What was that? Did he mean Coney Island? Was the damn man back
in New York? His breath stuttered out of him. He felt nothing, then
he did.

His closing thought: Why did Gray get on that bus two years ago? Why
had he left their lives?

DAUGHTER

    I don't know if he was ever here, on this spot in particular. I have
no information about where exactly he was, only that he did come here,
that small bit is certain, and that he was never heard from again. There's
hardly anybody on this island. I can't imagine what it was like all those
years ago, since it seems like places get more crowded as time passes,
not less so. There may have been no one at all. As I walk, I treat each
place like a place he saw: My dad was here on Corn Island and he was
thinking of me as he walked along the beach. He wanted to bring me

with him but I was too young. Mother wouldn't let him. I look into each face—not just here but everywhere—and I wonder, Could that be him? I have pictures but he could look like anyone by now. He could be somewhere doing the same thing, looking into the faces of young women and asking, Is it her? He could have gotten treatment, may still be alive, could have lost his memory, and could be sitting on the beach a kilometer away, knowing that he's missing something (me) but not knowing what it is, not able to put a word on it precisely, or an image. If there is anywhere he is, it is probably here, because time seems to have slowed on this island, so if he had a month to live someplace else it could have easily stretched into years and years on this island. I am standing with my feet just touching the water. I can imagine him.

In an earthquake, if trapped, the experts advise, do not light a match, do not move or kick, do not shout. Use a whistle or tap on a pipe.

Yes, one should always carry a whistle in earthquake country because you might be crushed under a building and not able to holler for help but only able to breathe lightly into your whistle. Or you might be buried alive under the bricks and have just enough air to toot, while your voice, should you have the strength to scream, is absorbed into the dust and paint. Or you might be flung far from civilization and have two broken feet so you can't walk back and two broken arms so you can't drag yourself over the dirt but you do have this handy whistle which, if you are too far to be heard and rescued, can be used as solo entertainment while you wait to slowly die.

So bring your whistle. Of course it is always possible that you wind up with your arm stuck under a slab of concrete so you can't reach the whistle (as Myers's arm is now), so it is best to keep the whistle in your mouth. No one with a whistle cuts an odd figure, though it may be difficult to speak with a whistle in your mouth. Not to mention, how are you supposed to eat with a whistle in the way? Or take a drink? Or sleep on your face? Advice: make someone else hold the whistle. But what if you don't have anyone else? What if you're all alone? In that case, sit with your whistle in your mouth. Don't eat or sleep. Don't examine the celebrated contents of your surroundings. Don't do anything. Wait for the earthquake. The earthquake is coming.

Chapter Ten

My dearest wife,

Today I saw collections of documents, works of art, phenomena described in books. I walked through the fields. I went to a town filled with more tourists than citizens—tourists sitting in seats, tourists rising to occasions, large tourists, small tourists, tourists frozen in an arabesque on the stairs.

As I am alive, I am your husband.

...was one way Myers could put it. Under the partition, tacked to the floor, he moved one finger as if to press Send.

More about Gray:

Did Gray reconcile with his wife when he left the city after spending some months at the bachelor's?

He didn't.

Where did he go?

Back to Syracuse. He settled down seventeen blocks from the spot of his original departure.

Why did he do that?

In order to stand by and take advantage of the rights bequeathed to him by the court: ninety-six hours divided in two and renewed monthly to visit with the product of his strife, a very small child, whom he first bundled in a blanket and carried home in the car, later picked up from the floor where she sat sucking her arm, and later led out by the hand.

His life was unsatisfactory. Sort of a half-life, really, decreasing in predictable segments, but he didn't complain because he loved the child in that wide, unknowable, impassioned, parental manner. It was for the sake of this small child that Gray saved his salary, purchased one squarish house (which Myers later sat in front of in vain, in rain), two welcome mats (front and back), one swing-set apparatus (sort of a federation of tubing and slats, which he unfolded, reconstructed, and depressed into the backyard in a spot where he could glimpse from the window the child tipping around on it if he was inside preparing a pudding snack). So it was.

Now Myers found he was in a conveyance, skirting the sides of walls, retreating. He couldn't recall what had happened. The accident had been shaken from his head. Patches of people and trees sucked away from him as if slingshot. Military trucks stood at the side of the road, dozens of soldiers milling around, growing smaller. His thoughts felt wrapped in blankets. What was he doing here? A straight line of green stood across the sky.

Now he seemed to be stretched out. He was buttoned-down, encased. He was being pushed on the floor through an entrance. There were noises that usually accompany chaos, but he stayed quiet in his straightwrap.

Frankly he was seriously grateful that someone was taking over the taking care of him. Whatever was going on, they'd have to handle him from here. He'd handled himself all these days, and it had been one mean week. He lay in his bracket. Bits of plaster dropped on his face. Someone nearby was saying something about units—people or blood. He had a thought rolling around: wasn't he supposed to meet Gray somewhere?

Somehow now Myers had been put into a wheelchair and left outside. He seemed to be in a parking lot or on some other paved space. He wasn't sure how he'd gotten here. Good God, what was this heat? His briefcase was there, seated on his lap. He had his sightseer equipment inside—his food kit, his hand sanitizer, his emergency shoelaces. His arm was fixed to a board. He sat and he watched the tourists hobbling around. He could see them, obviously foreigners with their pale hair and glasses. They were picking their ways around the wheelchairs, leaning over the cots to offer snacks and drink.

No, not tourists. He didn't know what they were.

What are you doing here? someone said, someone speaking English, standing over him.

Who, me? Myers started. Why? What happened?

It was a woman with a clipboard, a belt fashioned with hanging utensils.

Earthquake, she said.

Oh.

Is it just the arm and the ribs? she said.

He looked at himself. I guess so.

Any other injuries I should know about?

Not that I know of.

Any special conditions? Prior hospitalizations?

No, not since childhood.

And what was that?

Kid accident. You know, kids. Hit the head. He squinted up at her.

I see.

For two years after Gray left New York, he'd changed diapers, then soiled underwear, then green-kneed pants. He changed nothing else.

He'd spent the remaining six hundred and seventy-four hours of each month in automatic Laundromats, or in a blue, manual-transmission vehicle, or in front of a freshman college classroom where he solemnly recited grammar instruction four times a day on Mondays, Wednesdays, and Fridays, or in a parking lot removing boxed imperishables from a shiny wheeled cage and lowering them into his trunk.

Most people live this way. They really do.

What kind of M dots you go in for? she said.

Excuse me?

Malaria. Which kind are you taking?

(Somebody walked by in a spacesuit, or what looked like a spacesuit.)

Oh. None.

No malaria pills? She made a mark on her clipboard.

Do I need them?

Do you want to get incredibly sick every year for the rest of your life and die off slowly?

Myers considered. Not particularly.

Earthquake, yes, it was coming back to him now. There had been Christians, a church. An Internet café.

Do you think I could check my email? he said.

No.

It was spectacular the way those tourists were coming around. Figures appeared on the horizon with clothing tied around waists or looped over necks like capes. They carried implements, handfuls of bags or bottles, something to set out on the ground, chairs, sticks, shovels, axes. Here, a whole extended family, a grandmother and a grandfather in front, a little dog running to the side. There, one standing on top of a truck in a swimsuit, hand crooked to the sun.

Who are all these people? Myers said.

These are the volunteers.

Of course, he thought, volunteers, had to be. He could see that now.

And what are you? he said.

Another volunteer, she said. She was having a look at the ropy contraption around his arm. She worked at the knot.

Hey, what are you doing with that? he said. Leave that.

Here, this might hurt.

The pain came in a wave, dashed him into a faint, then staggered him awake.

I'd like to lie down. It's time to lie down.

Not enough stretchers, she said. Sorry.

Nearby, the volunteers pulled up their trousers, fastened on their shoes. They marched into the rubble of a building across the street. They waded to their waists. A very small volunteer ran up and down with a blue toy bucket. Two nuns raked rocks, or they may have been maids. Their black dresses billowed. Seagulls dotted the rocks. Somebody kept lifting a pup and tossing him away from the wreckage.

Do you think I could get some water? said Myers.

Someone will come around with it soon. Let me get this arm wrapped first. Then we'll do the ribs.

The arm on the board screamed for a long moment, then fell to a whimper.

I could use some water.

Soon. What did you say you were doing here?

Vacation.

Alone?

My wife joins in a few days, Myers said dryly.

Did you get your Typhim at least?

My what?

Bad. You can pick up typhoid anywhere. You can get typhoid just opening your mouth. You could have typhoid already. Hang on.

I believe my tetanus is up to date, for what it's worth, Myers gasped.

LOCAL NUN

This was a nothing earthquake, nothing. This was an earthquake I'll forget in a day. A few fallen tourists, a few hooked limbs. The last earthquake, now that was something. All the area families piled under the earth. We had to go out and get new ones.

Did you get your hep A, your Havrix?

No, I didn't get any of that.

Yellow fever?

No.

You better get on the stick, she said. How long do you think you're going to last here?

I'm not staying long.

Every day you last is a gift.

I've got nine more days to go.

This isn't Hannukah.

She was fumbling around down there. She was unknotting and turning. Dismantling. That hurt? she said.

A little. Myers thought that wasn't right but that may have been what he said. He didn't know what he said through the roar.

LOCAL NUN

It's not the biggest thing that happens in your life, an earthquake. You try to walk and you can't. You see people and you can't reach them. You try to scream and you can't hear your own voice. Then it stops.

You dig the people out, you set them back on their feet—lift by the shoulders, not the neck.

Late that night Myers would wake, hear a sound, think he heard a sound. Gray? he would say in the dark, the word coming out of his mouth. Gray? He switched on the lamp. No, he didn't. His arm gave a groan and he held still. There was no lamp beside him anyway because he wasn't at home, and he wasn't in the first hotel, or the second hotel, because he was in the hospital, and when he opened his eyes, which turned out to be shut, it was dim, not dark.

Late that night the sound wasn't Gray but it wasn't anything else either. There were sounds but they had nothing to do with him. The contents of the room—cots, people, pathways—spread out in regular intervals. He lay, the barrenness within him and the clutter without. A thought was pulling at him. It was just under the surface. He was forgetting something. It would come, he needed to wait. Out the window, the trees or whatever those were, bushes, the stack of housing, the ash and the human hum. Nearby were bodies taped to metal and given a wheel to steer. The utterly empty bottle of his soul. He waited for day.

Gray had ridden the bus to the city on the day of a cold February parade. He stayed for four and a half months, during which time his thoughts moved with the sluggishness of words being formed with alphabet blocks, one letter at a time, a small fat boy lining them up gracelessly. People move through that city with awe and expectation, but Gray felt nothing but oppression and pain, his interior arrangement a clogged river. He could see no future for himself. But he could not stay where he was. The despair wasn't over the marriage but the child. She was just over a year at the time he left, a little squiggle in a diaper.

How could you love something so small and for no other reason than that it belongs to you? He didn't know. He walked all over that city and each day he came back to the fact of her at one end of the state and him at the other. The news that came from the top half of the state was grim. Threats of only two supervised visits a year due to unfitness, mental abuse, his wobbling around with temp jobs.

His lawyer sighed on the phone. It's a woman's world, he said.

When at last Gray's thoughts organized into a simple sentence, it read: I can't lose that little girl.

So the day he got on the bus and left was not a day of defeat but of triumph. Without alerting anyone and without being told to, without a person on earth as witness (or so he believed), one afternoon instead of trolling around in circles and squares, he walked to the bus station and left, went back to fight for his daughter.

A man struggling in water looks somewhat like the inside of a jewel box or a crystal. The tiny bubbles shine whitely and sparkle. The more the man thrashes, the more it seems that gems and bits of silver and pearl are falling around him, as if he were caught inside a heavy opera costume, as if he were crashing through the stained glass of a cathedral, as if he were wrapped in air and light.

Chapter Eleven

MARIA

He turned up and checked in and that is it. He was already dying when he arrived. It wasn't what I did. He arrived late one day and hasn't left. At first he walked all over, went around town. I don't know where he went. Maybe he started dying after that. He doesn't speak any Spanish. Who knows what he's doing here. After a while he stopped walking and he got into bed and barely gets up. So I come in and turn on the light in the morning so he knows it's now day and it's time to keep his eyes open, and then I come in at night and switch it off so he knows it's bedtime and now he should sleep. That's my main job. My other job is to holler at my son to bring the poor man something to eat. If he found himself dying, wouldn't he at least want someone to come around with a sandwich now and then, or a cup of juice? Shame on him that I have to remind him.

I have no idea who he is or if he has anybody anywhere. The man is obviously just about dead. I called the doctor and the doctor hauled him over to the hospital. They put him in a cot and they said no doubt the man was dying, the good Lord knows he should be dead by now. What do you want to do with him? they said.

And I said, He's not mine. What do *you* want to do with him?

We aren't really in the business of caring for people in this dying way, they said.

We cure people, they said.

Apparently you don't, I said and pointed at him.

He's barely moving now. He gets his lunch, his snack, and in the evening I go out to the plaza. I find my son playing kick-stick and I say, Somewhere your father may be lying there like that at this very hour and you better hope someone's better than you are at bringing him a bowl of soup. Or I say, Let this be a lesson, son, about the cold heart, that a man could be left behind like this. Or I say, This is what becomes of a man who walks out on his family.

And my son says, How do you know that man has a family?

Every man has a family, I say, and there's only one reason a man leaves and that's for another woman.

And he says, Then where's the woman?

And I say, No woman stays with a man who left.

Chapter Twelve

Myers should leave her. That thought had formed in his mind. Her motives didn't matter. If this was the wife he'd got, he should just go, let her follow that man off a cliff.

But then one day Gray got on a bus and left. That's how the matter had ended.

Myers had watched it happen. Or, to be accurate, he watched her watch it happen, or watched her not be able to bring herself to watch it happen, watched her hide her face as the bus pulled away, actually roll her face to the wall, as if Gray was headed to war, as if Gray was the one who was her husband and was headed to a terrible war, a wrong war, one that we were losing, one that we could never hope to win, that a soldier could never hope to return from, every last man downed, grenaded or gassed, that's what she looked like when Gray got on the bus and that's what Myers, watching, wished was happening. What a tragedy. Oh woe.

How it happened was they all walked down to the station and only one of them bought a ticket and boarded a bus. The man leaves town with only a briefcase? Without even a sack of snacks for the ride? Yes, it's a little weird but who cares, there he went—the skeleton line for Syracuse, the bus backing up, Myers's wife weeping or being weepyish off to the side. At one point Gray looked out the window. Myers saw it: Gray seeing a woman, her head ducked against the wall, saw him study her momentarily—a woman making a minor spectacle of herself—before the bus dragged Gray away.

She walked away from the bus station, Myers behind. It was drizzly and her hair drew down her back. He couldn't see her face. She was just the figure in front of him and it fell to him to follow her, fallen woman, wet wife, low wife. And as for himself he had no picture in his mind, no image of himself heading down the street, a seedy undercover man in nightlight, no. He was absent, withdrawn. That was two years three months ago.

They walked back to the apartment and took up their lives. How else could it have wound up other than everyone back in their starting positions? Everyone back behind their pushcarts or rearranging their giftware, one of them keeping an eye out for any more anomalies and almost-affairs.

He kept expecting it to go back to like before, but it was never like before. "Before" wasn't like before. Even the early days took on a dark cast. She was an alien creature, this petulant, sad-mouthed thing.

After Gray rode away she came to a standstill. It took a near month because she was moving so fast, going around and around like a dropping kite, and what was Myers supposed to do other than worm behind her like the tail? But she slowed and slowed and finally did stop. And in the long pause before the fighting started up again in earnest, the woman seemed capable only of lying in bed and looking at the lighted people on the screen at her feet, and he, exhausted, not knowing what to do, so sick of it all you cannot imagine, unsure if he should leave or scream or what, sat down and watched with her.

They talked about the plots with the solemnity of idiot children trying to fit pieces into a dull brown puzzle. I hope they patch it up for the baby's sake, they said to each other, although they knew there was no baby, only a piece of wrapped cloth. Would the hero have his say, would the other hero give some mother something or other? Don't bet your last billion on it. Don't get short in the pants over it. And when they'd watched all the ones on TV, he went out and got more for them to watch and when he couldn't find any in the stores, he ordered more through the mail, downloaded them off the Net, and they, together in the bed, stared forward. They talked and talked and talked. Who knew if he still loved her, they said of some man who seemed to love or not love or love. Who knew if he could ever love again after what he'd been through.

I'm leaving, said Myers.

So am I, said another guy.

They were waiting at the hotel desk in Granada.

Yes, all that, walking in the rain, then the TV, then finally a fight, then another fight, then all the ones afterward, two years' worth, then her wanting to leave and his not letting her, then her wanting to leave again and his not letting her again, then his leaving at last, then the taxi in Syracuse, then all those airplanes and the accumulation of grit in his guts, then the earthquake and being carted around like a corpse, then the hospital bill and being sent back to the hotel, the entire town on emergency hold, a nagging sensation in his soul, his crooked arm bent in and ribs wrapped, and finally Myers himself, skidding, coming to a stop, here at the hotel checkout, a smooth counter in the middle of the Americas, and Myers stood (or leaned, rather), waiting to pay his bill and go back the other way because he didn't know what he wanted anymore but he knew it could not be here.

I'm going too, said the other guy. It was the guy from the other day, the one who didn't want to go outdoors, here he was, again at reception, still trying to check in or out, still, it seemed to Myers, Nicaraguan.

All I wanted was a vacation, he said.

Tell me about it, said Myers.

They went on like that for a while. The man who was obviously a Nicaraguan said it was a fine-looking place but there were spots just like it in Florida with better facilities too. Myers said he'd heard that and that he wasn't surprised, what with all the revolutions they had around here, what could one expect? Then the man who was obviously a Nicaraguan said he was amazed that they didn't at least *try* to do something about the mosquitoes, which were the size of *medium-sized dinosaurs*, and Myers said, And you can ask about the *live, smoking volcano* too. Had he heard about that volcano billowing smoke, practically exploding all over everybody, and they didn't even try to put it out? And the man who had to be a Nicaraguan said, The least they could do is clean the place up, clear away some of those wild plants. Put in some parks, lawn, rides.

Like an amusement park?

There you go. Tilt-a-Whirl. Coaster.

I hear you, said Myers. And what good is a place where a man can't even check his email, with earthquake volunteers hogging the computers?

They could make a fortune on their beaches, the man said. Ocean front and back and they've got nothing like a proper beach—just sand and water and sky.

Want to see a beach? someone said. It was a woman, the desk clerk. Her face was an angry scrawl, had had just about enough from these two.

And the man who was a Nicaraguan and not admitting it said, Who wants to know?

You want a beach, go to Corn Island. One hour plane ride, the most beautiful island in the world. Water like glass.

Not likely. I can only *ima*gine the restaurants.

The best.

Dancing?

Oh, dancing every night.

Tourists?

Everywhere. You can't get away from them.

What did they care for a charmless beach, a leafless line of sight? He and the guy beside him, each playing out their empty ancient parts. An island, nearly underwater, out on the sea, ready for the next big splash— hurricane, tidal wave, whatever—to come along at any moment, wash away the whole hurrah. Sure, why not be at the very edge when the havoc began? Why not be the first to sink, the first washed away, the first found bloated and floating? Corn Island? No, the only place these guys were headed now was home.

Just then, the wallpaper of Myers's heart tore off. Corn Island. That was it. He knew what had been shaken from his mind: *Meet me on Corn Island. The most beautiful island in the world.* Jesus, how could he have forgotten? The lobby took on a pearly cast and the people in front of him were shining facelessly, air paying out behind them in ribbons. Ladies and gentlemen, step aside. Myers was going to Corn Island.

I'll go, said Myers. Where is it?

They turned to him, surprised.

On the Atlantic.

He wasn't sure exactly which way that was from here. He shrugged one shoulder. Which way is that? May as well go right now, he said.

Oh yeah? said the other guy. With an arm like that? Looks like you got banged up all right.

This is nothing. Myers waved at the bandage. I've had worse falls than this.

I'd believe that.

A beach might be just the thing right now, said Myers.

I've got nothing special on, said Myers. Nothing I have to file in for. How do I get there?

Hell, the man said. Maybe I'll go too. He held out his hand. My name's Spoke.

So what would they do on Corn Island, the most beautiful island in the world? What a question! They'd stay in the most expensive hotel, of course. The tallest, the grandest, the one with the best restaurants.

Where somebody brings drinks out to you on the beach.

And there's an Internet café.

And a bar in the swimming pool.

Dinner tonight will be my treat.

No, my treat.

No, my treat!

We'll both treat. We'll have two dinners.

And two breakfasts in the morning.

Myers gasped and gripped his side, could not expand with joy.

You don't look so good, Spoke observed.

It was brilliant having this Spoke fellow along. The perfect decoy. *I was nowhere near the guy. My buddy Spoke will tell you. I was here by the pool all day.* It would take nearly nothing to pull it off. The guy naps for a bit or wanders off after some girl. Myers wouldn't need long once he found Gray. *Hey, Spoke, you woke up. Look, I got you another drink.* He could buy a good knife in any snorkel shop. He could buy a gun.

Gray, it's time to pay up.

Island vacation associations: beach bag, bathing suit, drink on the beach, bodysurfing, sandcastles, seasick, seashell, beached body, volleyball, pier rot, water swallow, seaweed, rot stench, blood water, drown kit, glacier melt.

The desk clerk had something to say in Spanish. She said it so fast, Myers didn't catch it.

She needs your card back, Spoke said, because he understood. She needs to run it again.

Myers handed the card back and the desk clerk ran it again.

(Another consideration: any wife in the Americas wouldn't put her nose up at an island beach. Were there direct flights from JFK? Not likely, but she could fly direct to Managua, then to this Corn Island place.

First the phone call to make the reservation—or she could do it online. First the Internet, then the taxi. Don't forget your passport! Myers shouted to her across the continent. Don't forget! First plane, second plane, taxi. She wouldn't need much luggage. She wouldn't need more than a change of clothes. They'd buy new things on the island. The luggage could be carry-on, pull-on. He'd take care of Gray once and for all. Next, island vacation with wife. It could happen.)

The card does not work, the desk clerk was saying now in English.

It works, said Myers.

It does not work.

Spoke looked away.

Here, try this one.

The desk clerk took the second credit card.

This card does not work either, she said.

A sunlit beach hung on a poster, the color of a fine layer of sawdust.

The machine doesn't work, said Myers.

The machine says to hold the card.

I'm going to go ahead and get a cab, said Spoke. He had his suitcase in his hand.

Could you please come this way? said the desk clerk.

The machine is broken.

Since I'm done, Spoke said, I don't want to make a cab wait.

The clerk was drawing a line across the air. This way, sir.

Why, as Myers stood there, did this moment suddenly come back to him? His mind was flipping through cards. He recalled an early disappointment, then an earlier one. His days had been slipshod, taped-together things for so long, he forgot when they had seemed whole, but he stopped on this moment. It was before their marriage, before they'd even moved in together. They'd picked a place, were packing. He was excited, being funny, dancing around, saying, This is great! I don't know why everyone doesn't do this, fall in love, get married, ha ha.

I don't know why everyone does, she said.

It's fun, said Myers. That's why.

Fun? she said. What's fun about it? She had a half-wrapped glass in her hand. She wasn't laughing.

What did it mean? Myers saved that moment in his heart, returned to it in the years of his marriage because it seemed to express her completely. She'd always been a stranger. Unknowable in more ways than most.

I'll need to call my wife, he said.

The next moment Myers was walking over the tile, going at a city-man pace across the lobby, escorted by members of the management, his arm burning and cracking, his side aching, through a group of soccer players sitting around on their duffs, Myers weaving through them and emerging.

If he had known it would be this easy to phone her, he might have done it days ago. Turned out all he had to do was be hit by an earthquake, mutilate a limb, settle the repair bill, have no money left over. In a case like that, they'll take care of the call home for cash. All you do is sit in your plastic slot and take the phone when they wave at you—the wave meaning: She's on the phone. By God, your wife is on the phone.

He took the phone and said, I am having a credit card misunderstanding.

I meant to tell you about that, she said.

SPOKE

There was obviously something wrong with the man—and I mean
besides the head, which wasn't so bad as Elephant Man, but noticeable.
He seemed friendly enough, but I wasn't about to pay his way or have a
financial liability along. This week has been trying enough. I felt a little
bad leaving him there, but one cannot care for every stone on the path.
It was a pretty sad affair.

Did you cancel the credit cards in the middle of my vacation?

Cancel, no. I did not cancel them.

Did you phone and say, "Please cancel"? I believe there is a word for
that and that word is "cancel."

I'm sorry, really I am

You're sorry? Did it happen by accident? Did you trip over the credit
card plug?

Your plane ticket cost a fortune, she said.

And no, she said. I did not cancel exactly.

SPOKE

People are fakers—that's all we do. Can you think of anything you
do that's not done for the precise reason of pretending to be something
you're afraid you're not? Still, I don't believe he was lying, that it was
all a scam. He seemed genuinely surprised. But then, one never knows.
Either way, that is not the sort of person to wait around for, what with
so much wrong with him just pasted on like that for all to see, and then
to find more lurking below within ten minutes of meeting him. There
are limits.

Who buys a same-day ticket out of the country? she said. I'm sure I never heard of that, and if I did I would laugh.

I'm on vacation.

Vacation doesn't begin the same day you decide it.

Sometimes.

No, never. Nobody does that. You wait, you suffer.

I waited, I nearly died of pain.

Nearly dying is not vacation.

As it happens... said Myers and stopped. (No sense in looking like a wimp about it.)

And it's certainly not a vacation if you don't have a job to go back to. The receptionist called, by the way. They're sending over your personals.

Then it hit him as if his mind were a small round hollow place into which a ball could come flying and here came that ball.

Oh no, said Myers. You reported the credit cards stolen.

Immediate tragedies not about Myers: the tragedy of the light in the room, the tragedy of the lit things, and the lit people, the tragedy of the movement in the building, the tragedy of the slow drip somewhere dripping, the tragedy of time, the tragedy of two voices, the tragedy of sound, the tragedy of...

You just had to make your point. You just had to buy the most expensive ticket anybody ever heard of.

Do you understand that now my return ticket is no good?

You yourself wouldn't blame me if you were in your right—

Do you understand that now I can't go home?

I ask you, who pays three thousand dollars just to get off the ground?

...the tragedy of the sidewalk outside, the tragedy of the rooster (unseen but heard), the tragedy of the sun, the tragedy of many motors, many, passing and passing on the street, the tragedy of the many lives running around out there, the tragedy of the buds that fight through the hard earth and of the rain that crushes them, the sun that burns the leaves...

He hung up the phone and he could hardly face Nicaragua.

That was his first thought: *I can hardly face this country.* His face was turned to it, yes. Any way he turned, his face was pointing at this country, some piece of it, but hardly, and then the second thought, which followed like a rolling bead, was not a thought, but a feeling, so overwhelming that it took over. He felt like a verb, not a man—like falling water, emptying houses, slowing heartbeats, something thickening, drying up, or wetting down, getting heavier or scaling off, stripping away. He felt himself coming off in strips, becoming matted, smelly, dense, and the sound inside him was a shout and he could feel it around his ears and eyes, the tingle of it, this knowledge: she wanted to leave him here.

...the tragedy of air, its emptiness, its abundance, its decay as it enters and exits bodies, the tragedy of water, its weight, its aimless wanderings over the world, the tragedy of its scarlessness, of being unmarkable, unremarkable.

Now the management was all over there discussing what to do about him. They were going to have to do something, they certainly were. They were buzzing away, shaking their heads and nodding. They'd have to get this one squared away all right. He sat where they put him, on the other side of reception, his belongings in a heap beside him. They stood in their huddle, had never heard of such a thing. Oh, the people they'd call about this one. He'd tried this one out on them: Bill me. Ha. Did he think this was communism? Free holidays for all? We don't have any communism here anymore. The gringo pays. The gringo always pays.

Meanwhile Myers took up his briefcase and walked away.

Ran.

THE UNTRAINER

Corn Island, yes, I've been here for, what, six weeks. What's it like? Well, it has a sea full of oysters and a tow like a lung, that sort of pucker and suck. Down by the coral and reefs, there's the usual battery of fish swatting up and down. Above the sea? Sand, that's about it. Nobody'll find any ancient civilizations under these dunes. No old pots and pans, tablets, no bus fare. No one used to be here who isn't. Other than this dolphin, there's not much to look at. There's nothing here worth wadding up and bagging. Nothing I'd want to pluck off a tree.

A few pieces of information Myers would like to have about Gray:

Is Myers the only goddamn person on the planet stupid enough to be looking for Gray?

(No.)

Is anyone lucky or unlucky enough to know where goddamn Gray is other than Gray?

(Gray does not know where Gray is.)

Just what did the guy think he was doing, leaving the country like that anyway?

(Sometimes a man seeks a runway.)

Myers did not know this, but Gray was not on Corn Island the day Myers fled his bill. Gray had never been to any part of Nicaragua and never would. He would die not having seen its wet sky.

On the day Myers found himself at the edge of an earthquake, Gray was installed in a very hot town named David, pronounced "Dah-*veed*," second syllable stressed. The town was two countries away, in Panama of all places.

The town of David stood halfway between mountain and beach (as

114

one always is in Panama unless one is already sitting on a mountain or a beach). One of the town's few distinctive features was the variety of clocks tacked to the wall of the bus station. Another was the scatter of public Internet cafés. A dollar an hour. Not bad.

Gray had not deliberately deceived Myers. He believed he was in Nicaragua, and he waited for Myers as one waits for spring, with eagerness but skepticism. The mix-up arose from an innocent mistake. Gray had always meant to see the sights of Central America—a place not so far that the season flipped over or the time went askew, but not so close as to not be foreign (Canada ought to be a little ashamed of itself, really). So one fine Sunday afternoon Gray landed in Panama City (home of the historic canal and other celebrated graveyards, nice holiday spot)—that much he had straight. He disliked the city comprehensively, took a bus to a town called Boquete, where it rained and shined at the same time like a scene from the endtimes and the wind blew like a threat. He disliked it too and decided the next day to go to Nicaragua (fine place for any former socialist, he'd had his Lenin days in college). He traveled to the border (two buses), crossed legally into *linda* Costa Rica, with plans to ride on to Nicaragua. He went into a border store with the intention of buying provisions for the next leg of the trip. The store happened to be very large and long. It straddled the border, one end opening into Pana, the other into Costa, like two ends of a fish, and Gray spent so long picking through the shelves that he got turned around and wound up walking out the wrong door into Pana again, a slip he never discovered. He simply got back on a Panama bus, rode to the end of the line, got off in the town of David. He checked into a hotel and called it Nicaragua.

He knew it wasn't Costa Rica by simple deduction. The hot, cramped town he found himself in couldn't be in Costa Rica—no tourists for one thing, and everyone knows you can't go to Costa Rica without stepping on a tourist and seeing it skitter off. Plus, the place wasn't beautiful. It had its charms, as Gray discovered over time (the top half of the town:

the sky, what one could see of it, and the bird-filled trees in the *centro*).
He'd never been, strictly speaking, an observant fellow, but it looked
nothing like the brochures of Costa he'd seen.

Gray didn't figure out his mistake, not because he spoke no Spanish
and never learned more than a few words (which happened to be the
case), but because, unknown to Myers or even to Gray himself, Gray was
suffering from a massive and growing brain tumor. His functions were
deteriorating, the flow of oxygen slowing. He was becoming widely
disoriented. The happiness he thought he felt may have been pain, and
his longings had likely been fulfilled long ago.

Few people knew about the cancer. Gray and Myers did not number
among them. Gray's ex-wife did. She still had the privilege of being
listed as the emergency contact in Gray's medical files, so it was she who
received the call from the doctor, after the doctor tried to reach Gray
at home two days after he had (quixotically, blurrily) left the country.
Gray had gone to the doctor because of his symptoms (hearing loss,
dizziness, confusion), but it was the ex-wife, not Gray, who heard the
results of the MRI.

So this was known to the ex-wife and eventually to Gray's small
daughter, who would one day grow up and go to Nicaragua in search of
her father.

SPOKE

I was settling into a taxi—this was about twenty minutes later. I had
to wait outside on the steps. This is the kind of place where any time,
day or night, you put out your hand and there's a taxi at the curb. In
this one way it is like New York (except you don't raise your hand like
a salute, you keep it low and you point to the spot where you want the
taxi to be), and it is also like New York in the fact that in any emergency
there is no taxi anywhere ever. As soon as the quake hit they were gone
and had to be coaxed back like kittens. So I waited for twenty minutes
or so and when I finally got one, I slid in my suitcase, I slid in beside

it, everything was fine. I had an elbow up on the back of the front seat and I was just saying, Get me out of here immediately, Managua airport, please—because I was going home, forget it.

Suddenly I saw that crazy man run out of the building.

Nobody else saw, I don't think. He broke from the hotel, pushed out the doors, went down the steps, charged off, broken arm and all. In his other hand he carried what seemed to be an honest-to-God briefcase. Amazing. A photograph or a painting, say, might capture the heroism or cowardice of that moment.

On this trip so far I have seen many strange things. Each step, there's a new stone on the path to choose not to care for. So when I saw that man run out of the building and into the trees, I leaned back in the taxi, let the air-conditioning cool my mind.

Wait, scratch that, I said. You know this place, Corn Island? How do I get there?

Look, there are hundreds of other people, thousands, really, all over town and beyond, all over the world even, millions of them, billions. They're just lying around or propped up somewhere, or they're trying to get in at the gate, so many they can't all fit in one place and they can't get enough ceilings or roofs or tarps to cover them. There are too many people and not enough tarps, you hear about how the tarps keep blowing off and there's not enough food or the food is in the wrong place and people can't figure out how to move it and people are starving. You wouldn't believe what some of these people are doing. I don't see what the difference is if one man isn't where he's supposed to be. He just cleared a little space. One fewer body to tend and shuttle. I wasn't going to be the one to tattle. What did I care when I was headed to the most beautiful island in the world? That's how I see it.

In the case of a man in water (Myers or someone else), it might be hard to distinguish play from strain. The man's busy hand signals could be in fun, not panic. Frenzied gestures—much like a fish flapping on the pier—could be in jest. It only becomes clear once the long sink begins, the down-going, the drowning, the getting to the bottom of it. From above it is simply what we see every day: objects dropping, shrinking, fading, just another thing getting away from us, so what. From underneath it looks like the body is not falling but like it's coming on, bearing down, shooting off bubbles, one arm swinging, the entire gathering speed, closing in, growing larger, should be put a stop to.

Chapter Thirteen

CLAIRE

My father could twist your arm off, I shouted.

The bartender blew on a glass, rubbed it

He's the greatest dolphin trainer who ever lived! I said.

That's a step up from being a clown, someone said.

The line of men beside me looked like they'd been locked into their stools with a wrench. I had my skinny elbows up on the counter. I had my skinny butt on the stool. I had my skinny skirt over my knees, my last skinny bucks in my hand. The sun was going down, putting a scrape in the haze. Out the window was Chicago—streets of four-flats washed up from the lake and dried out on a flatland of convenience stores. My hair was a staticky knot from a night on the train and my clothes were frilly with wrinkles. Two dogs sat on the sidewalk, waiting for me to come out. I could see them. This day had been so long, it seemed like it should have been over for hours by now, like I should have been able to slash two from the calendar. I'd even gained an hour in Indiana.

I brought out the photo, put it on the bar. The bartender picked it up.

You know him? he said.

I've never seen him in my life.

He shook his head, laughed.

What? I said.

You don't read the papers? Go to the show?

No.

Well, he *is* the greatest dolphin trainer who ever lived, he said.

Really? I said. I took the photo. He's my dad.

THE UNTRAINER

I was born underwater. My mother wove seaweed baskets for the Mexican ships in the Gulf. Say what you want, a job's a job. She worked in water, the long hours of the poor, so all I heard was sea sounds for nine months. She did not get Labor Day off—there's a shameless asshole overman for you. I washed out of her womb and the foreman had me fetching starfish by the time I was five. I never knew my father. My mother told me nothing and I wasn't going to ask. Some water-dog prick, no doubt. Nothing manly in leaving your egged-up woman behind. As soon as I was old enough, I went to Cancún, where I grew up against a skyline of sails. I dove with the dolphins for tourists who threw coins that I caught in my fist.

One day I came out of the water and onto the hard earth of Mexico. I took buses clean across the country, from the Atlantic to the Pacific, through the cities and towns, the ruins, the rivers. When I got to Mazatlán, I took a boat through international waters around Baja and over the border. I walked up onshore and into California. Hollywood felt brittle under my feet and the smog kept the air cool.

No, I wasn't after some minor-league American dream—TV, savings, packaged applesauce, frequent-mile flying. You think there's something special about that? Let me be the one to tell you: You've got nothing special going on in the States.

No, I went to find someone.

Place was bigger than I thought.

I got a job training dolphins for the movies, the movies where the dolphin saves the kid but almost doesn't. The movies where the dolphin almost dies but doesn't. Where the mother smiles like the one you have at home, the one who almost never smiles but when she does she almost looks like that. Where the father pals around like no father ever does anywhere. That sort of thing, that's what I threw in with.

Sure, I pulled a little stunt on the side. I was the guy with the underwater gun, the guy swallowed by the whale, the one who fell to the deep tangled in a net so the stars could sit around and eat carrot cake up top. I blew off the tip of my thumb. I shattered my cap. That stunt shit is for cowards. But many lives are carried out that way. I wasn't going to be the first to complain. That's a rule you can live by.

I preferred to work with the fish.

CLAIRE

You've seen these movies? I said to the guys. You're sure it's him? These are confirmed sightings?

Of course, they said. Movies and shows. You turn on the TV, anything with tots and sea mammals splashing across the screen, your father did it, they said.

These boys had grown up on those shows. Without him, they assured me, the dolphins would have swum away years before.

This is interesting, I thought. This is like finding out your sandbox is the seashore. Like your bathtub is the sea. Very interesting. This is like finding out somebody stole your sandbox, which turned out to be the seashore, took it away bucket by bucket, and now everyone in the world is over there making castles in it, lying on it in the sun.

Neat.

THE UNTRAINER

Then I had a conversion. It's the best conversion story you ever heard. That's why I can't tell it to you unless you pay me ten bucks. For ten bucks I give you the book and you read it. I don't have time to tell it all again. A man could spend a life telling stories.

A conversion story? It's like any story about a thing that stops doing one activity and starts doing another—like a season changing cycles or an animal dying off. It happened twelve years ago, after I'd trained every dolphin Hollywood had ever seen, played funnyman to the octopi.

Why did I stride over to the other side, leave my movie-making ways and means? Oh, come on. That's a really stupid question. You ever see a chicken lock a person in a box? You ever see a bear make a human dance on a ball? You ever see a dog make a man beg? I know what it is to have a human heart and to know what is in it.

CLAIRE

The men wanted to know: had my father taught me to train? They were feeding bills into the music box. They were balling up napkins.

No, I said for the millionth time.

Are you sure? Are you sure? they said. What a shame, what a waste, they all agreed. My father was the best the world had ever seen, they said, and now he didn't train anymore. Shame his talents weren't passed on.

He's a nutcase now, they said. A terrorist or something.

That's wonderful, I said. That's great news.

THE UNTRAINER

I steal dolphins. I track them, I follow them out of the water from where they've been captured, follow their wet bloody prints to their prisons—their pools, their parks, their zoos. I kidnap them in the night or I burst in with henchmen and take them at gunpoint. I call it a rescue. The papers called it, let's see, vandalism, as if the dolphins were a can of paint, or environmentalism, like bringing back your tinfoil, or terrorism, the kind of terrorism where you save the innocent and set them free.

The rescue is the easy part. The hard part is the untraining. You can't just drop them into the sea and expect them to swim off triumphantly. You think you'd be fine if someone dumped you out onto some vast plain, no map, no cellphone, no ticket? They're like anything else. You have to bring them home.

Once I have a dolphin or two, I bring them to deserted islands or almost-deserted islands like this one. I put up some nets in the ocean like the ones you see here—these nets and sticks. They protrude from the water. I build a hut out of thatch at the ocean's rim. That's for me. Then I have to ignore the dolphins. Sometimes it takes weeks. Sometimes months. We have to sever the tie between animal and man. I spend all day and night here, except once a day I trudge over the sand dune and under the incredible sun with my hat and my water and the dogs (dogs follow me everywhere, always have) to civilization or whatever dumbed-down version of it is closest. I get what I need—fish for them, water for me—and go back. I walk along my own line of footprints, following myself there and back. There are no variations, no detours. I am well-thumbed.

I stay as long as it takes. The dolphin goes back and forth and I go back and forth and after a while I begin to feel trapped, like I'll never get away, I'll always be alone, far from home, among strangers who don't speak my language, and the loneliness feels like a choke chain. In moments like that I am tempted to simply lift the net before they're ready, let everyone wander over the earth, each according to their nature, the dolphin in water, me on sand or concrete or grass. Why not?

And it isn't just these little pony acts I break up. I also go to places on the other side of the earth where fishers empty their nets, drop the dolphins on the docks, and hack them to bits, toss them aside. I go underwater, cut their lines, explode their boats. I leave the fishers notes. *The next slice you make on a dolphin will be matched on the anatomy of your wife.* I slash their bedding, clothing, whatever dumb-eyed pet happens to be at hand, as a visual example for the illiterate. I do my best, but there is far too much evil in the world for one person to counter.

You think it's easy doing what I do? Let me ask you—you think what you do is hard? Think about it. Is what you do hard? My guess is yes. What I do is harder.

CLAIRE

No, I've never seen the shows. No, I've never seen his picture in the paper. Never heard of him. Never watched the shows. I don't read a lot. I don't watch TV. The truth is I have no sense of my mother. And I don't know who this man was either. Even the man who raised me— how did he do it, knowing I wasn't his? I don't know these people or what I was to them. The proof of their connection to me is scant, is practically nonexistent. No one on the outside looking in at me would see it. But I inspect them in my mind, I study them for any sign, any trace or hint that could illuminate. I would take any reasonable explanation.

He's in Central America right now, the guy next to me said. I saw it on the news.

He left the country, I said. Okay, fine.

Go to one of those animal-rights groups, said the bartender. Go tomorrow. They'll know him. They'll know how to contact him.

I tipped the drink to the photo. One thing that man does not need, I said, is a daughter.

THE UNTRAINER

No, I don't miss Hollywood. God, no. I didn't care about the cash. Oh, I know people do, all right. Halfwits on the ukulele earn a coin. A lineup of jingles, a few strings tied to a post, you got a peso in your hand. I have nothing to do with that. I'm an untrainer, not a circus.

I only went to the States in the first place to find a woman I had fallen in love with. I met her in a Cancún resort. She didn't want me. She was married with a kid last I heard. That was a long time ago now. Sure, I've had others. It's a bad life to do alone. But no one wants to lead the kind of life I have to lead. I'm a solo show.

After this release, I'm off to New York. There are two at Coney Island I need to fetch. They're shutting the place down. Guy there called me on the sly. Said I better get them out while I can.

CLAIRE

Pour me another, I said. I held out my glass. I'm dying of thirst over here.

Slow down, the bartender told me. You want to die? Keep drinking like that.

He swiped the bar with a rag.

He doesn't know you're here, that's all, the bartender said. How could he know?

I didn't say this to the bartender, but my mother was a TV star. Her life was not private. And they were even in the same business. My father knew I was there.

Don't you want to meet him? He'd be easy to find.

Hey smart guy, I said. Hey genius. I held out my glass. All I want is another one of these.

You know how it is to want something. Desire builds like a little house in your head and it sits there, half-constructed in your mind. Women who want children are this way. Artists are this way about pictures. It doesn't go away. You may forget for a few months but then it's back, the unfinished pieces of what you want.

I don't want to want anything. I'm fine.

I could hardly move my head.

There was a man on the train with a broken brain, I was saying.

All right, said the bartender. Okay.

Okay, I said. Okay, okay, okay, okay.

When the bartender leaned over, I pulled him in and shut his mouth with mine.

I don't recall leaving the bar. A slow fog settled in over the long horizon of the counter. The stools turned like boats on the water. The men bobbed away. The next thing I knew I was lying in a light, in a warm envelope of brightness. There was a thrumming sound nearby. For a moment I thought I'd died and that these were my final moments floating in the holy sunrise and it was as nice as everyone says. Then the old will to live stepped in: Don't let me be dead, it said. What a tired thought.

I opened my eyes. I was on a paisley spread, the bartender in the bed, my head dissolving like a sugar cube.

It doesn't matter if he knew about me. You know how is best? Just knowing he's out there. My real dad. He is perfectly formed in my eye. Nothing has gone wrong. There have been no arguments, no misunderstandings, no doubts that he might have about me have come up. And I haven't seen anything I don't like either. I haven't begun to lose him in any way at all.

I got up. The radiator ticked like a time bomb. I found the bartender's wallet. I took enough to get home. I took more, I took the rest. I got dressed. He raised his head and I gave it a pat. I went. I got back on the train and headed for New York.

I am weary of my adventure.

THE UNTRAINER

So this dolphin here, he comes originally from far out in the ocean off the coast of Corn Island. We tracked the trainer. I had the help of automatic weapons and men. We followed him into the hills straight to the dolphin, brought him here. I called the local authorities and they came over and threw a salaried, half-hour fit and said I had to give him back. Then I called the international authorities and they came over and threw another fit, a bigger fit, a tantrum of the leisured rich. And now, as an expression of new national interest in the perishing paradise and hope for a swimmy future for all and for better relations with all animal bodies and especially with the international financial body, the national authorities have congratulated me and have invited everyone to witness this spectacular media event. We will all go together, all the authorities, as one happy group, to take the dolphin home. The untrainer will go one way and the dolphin another.

This is the kind of shit I put up with to see one animal free.

Hey, get away from the animal.

Chapter Fourteen

Here is the wife's confession, which she spoke aloud but not to her husband. Myers never heard it and never knew. She confessed to a stranger, not the same one she'd followed, but a third man in a third suit, also with a briefcase, though she never saw him carry it, never saw the briefcase in the air at all. She saw it on a desk, jaws open, and she could not view its contents from where she sat, though she supposed them to be not entirely unlike the contents of the briefcases of other men she'd known, husband, strangers, and so on.

She told the third man her story, meted it out with the disimpassioned face of a dashboard, and then rode home on the train. She did this each week, the same man, same hour and day, same story, and each time she paid him the same sum of money to listen to her confession, and not to judge or scold her, but merely to murmur phrases in a detached tone or to ask a simple question softly and from behind a lifted hand so that she could not hear him even if she leaned forward and cocked her head to his voice. She confessed for twelve weeks, as her benefits allowed, and then she stopped.

Confession to follow.

The confession began: Once I ran away from my husband.

THE WIFE'S CONFESSION (PART I)

I ran away from my husband once. I was gone for so short a time that he never found out I'd gone. It was winter. We'd gotten married only a few months before. The toaster was still shiny and reflective. We were still perfecting our recycling program. I was still writing out our thank-yous on ivory paper.

How he and I met was nothing special. On my end, it had something to do with college, with being a few years out of it. I'd made it all the way through school without any big loves, just the odd boyfriend and Valentine's date. I'd seen enough of my parents' marriage—two corpses feigning life—to keep me off romance. My father had some kind of wire arrangement around his heart, a dark armor that clanked when he walked. He seemed most absent when present. He spoke exclusively in the imperative. Don't touch the thermostat. Use your napkin. Tiptoe. The worst was when he added his special word on the end, his concession to the single hour of therapy my mother had insisted on. No stomping, *friend.* Shake hands with Mr. Clark, *friend.* Other than these clipped commands, he was completely silent. His smile was so phony it looked painful.

I can see now that my mother was unhappy, that she walked through my growing years bewildered and depressed, but as a child I took it as disinterest, so I returned the same. By the time I was a teenager, we all politely disliked each other with the same chilly restraint.

So I graduated, set off for the city, found a job. There I was, pretzeled into my seat on the subway, and who should come strolling over like a cowboy. I think it was the most spontaneous thing he'd ever done, the way he approached me, and therefore the most spectacular, and although there wasn't anything spectacular about it, it seemed spectacular to me.

He sat down next to me. I am having the moment, he said, that I've always heard about.

Where you miss your stop and wind up in Queens? I said.

Where I meet the woman I will love.

The next year was like nothing I'd known. More than a cowboy, he was like a fireman or some other dependable community service. He was steady, able, good with his hose (ha), and my reaction was appropriate: I was relieved. I had never been close to anyone, not really, and I wanted to try. I imagined closeness as being like the people I saw in restaurants and on TV, people with clean faces, with problems like mathematic equations, which could be solved with a pencil and a sharp mind. It was the strangest time in my life. I felt something in me healing. Yes, I thought. It could be that simple. This nice man. I could love him. He could save me.

Save me, I thought.

I have almost no memories from that year. It's not that I feel nothing for it, it's just that it hurts too much to look at. I see a blur of objects— my dresses like straitjackets, the prehistoric pasta we cooked off his shelf. There was the Halloween we worked the haunted house—a swarm of children in homely Kmart costumes, plastic green pants, face masks. We made love on the floor of his office. We made love on his desk. We went exploring, found a machine junkyard and picked our way through the scraps and curled metals. I was amazed at how easy everything was when I had someone beside me saying, Good job!

Saying, Wow, you look great doing that.

Saying, Here, let me get it!

The truth is, it wasn't the cure. I slowly became aware of this. The infection was still inside me and it had been hacked back but was once again growing.

I remember as a child waiting for my parents to soften. I looked for signs, weak points in their armor to push on and break through. But my mother had given up, had sunk into herself. She fended me off from deep inside her stronghold. My father may have never felt a thing in his life, for all I know. I waited. Inside, my mind was a windswept plain, a few stalks of thistles, rocks, and it stayed that way. Now with this new man around, I was trying desperately to redecorate, drag in couches over the fields of my mind, put up some paintings with clothespins, attach them to the lines.

The truth is I was having little doubts even at the courting stage. (What did he have to be so helpful about?) (Did he have to be cheerful every goddamn minute?) (Honestly now, what was there about me to like?)

I have no idea what my parents' great disappointment was.

Maybe each other.

Maybe me.

We had a crazy Technicolor wedding. We moved into an apartment, took out of boxes a game show's worth of appliances, began our marriage.

Then the real trouble began.

Myers pushed through the doors, fled the hotel management. He had one hand clenched around the grip of his briefcase, the other pinned patriotically to his chest. Outside, the streets were full. Across the street the park was full, a numberless noisy crowd, his eardrums raw and banging. He went down the steps and into the hotel garden.

THE WIFE'S CONFESSION (PART II)

I had assumed it was a birth deformity. How else does a head get that way? I didn't mind, that's how love is—you accept what they're born with. Sure, I realized he wasn't aware of it. From the mirror's flat face, he couldn't see the way it was misshapen, and no one had told him. I wasn't going to be the one to break the news. I do have manners, if little else. One day I was doing some wifely arranging (*not* snooping) and I found the hospital papers in his files. One sheet described the accident. There'd been witnesses, corroborations. From the ground below, from windows across, they had seen him. A young man stepping up into a window frame, leaping out.

You tell me: what sort of man jumps out the window?

That first night I sat up and watched him sleep, only his earlobe visible over the blankets. I don't know what I was more upset about: that he had chosen not to tell me or that this man I had entrusted myself to, had gone so far as to marry, this man had thrown himself out the window, had nearly killed himself, had certainly tried, had a death wish or a wish to fly or some other deeply irregular desire. Why hadn't he told me? How was I supposed to believe him now that I knew what was in his heart? How was he supposed to save me?

I am a private person but at this point I needed to talk. I went to my closest friend, Anita. I told her everything. She was unimpressed.

So? she said.

He was twelve, she said. What won't a kid do?

Jump out a window? she said. That's nothing. You should hear what *my* husband did before we met.

Every man has a weakness, she said. Every man has a past.

I said, Here's what I want to know. Is it contagious?

What on earth? she said. It's not the plague.

I don't want to get it.

Your head's not going to cave in, she said. Get what?

Not the dent, I said. The urge.

Myers ran through the garden, along the sun-washed, white-spilled wall of the hotel. Flowers were bunched in the way, strewn in maniac obstacle clumps. He veered around them, vaulting when he had to. He came to a gate at the end of the garden—padlocked. He could possibly squeeze through.

He drew himself up, squeezed through.

THE WIFE'S CONFESSION (PART III)

I don't know, I don't think it's so weird. I can think of any number of reasons. Humans, we just hop out of things, off things. We splatter ourselves in inappropriate places. Because we have nothing to live for.

Because we want to destroy what we can.

Because we want to be something we can't.

Because we don't really believe we can die.

I'd been unhappy for a long time. I had been counting on him to be strong. I didn't want to be close to someone with secrets and a fake smile, someone ready to jump. I have that already, I've had it.

I have had it.

The next few days I struggled. I was surprised he had it in him to pull off such a stunt and that he had the restraint to hide it. How could someone like him do it? He was more cunning than I'd imagined. Part of me thought I was being unfair. I should confront him, demand an explanation. Then it occurred to me: was I using this as an excuse not to love him? In the kitchen I watched him work the can opener. I watched him arrange the jars. What was behind that face of his? Of mine? An eeriness crept over me and hardened me. All I could do was look at him a little more stone-hearted each day and feel, inside, stone.

Myers crabwalked down the street as fast as he could, gasping and sweating, a roar in his ears, a pain in his side. He stepped over the cracks. The earth's slick human protective covering was coming off in places now, not the whole thick thing, just the upper layer, peeling off, unsticking, to reveal whatever was pulsing and suffocating below. He stopped, craned his head around the corner and down the avenue, could see the hotel and a long line of figures stringing out of the building, fanning into the street. He couldn't believe it. They were coming after him.

SPOKE

Why did I come to Nicaragua? Mostly to visit my grandmother. I just came from there. I would have seen my grandfather too except he's been dead six years, which no one bothered to tell me. How hard is it to send a note? I haven't seen either of them in twenty years or many of my other relations either, because when I was twelve years old I was drafted into the army of the revolutionary government and I walked out of our town with all the other soldiers and I haven't been back until now.

THE WIFE'S CONFESSION (PART IV)

Finally I left one morning. He was gone, weekend with the parents. I didn't leave a note and I planned not to come back. I took only a few items—several sandwiches of cheese, a change of slacks. I closed the door to the apartment and walked away.

I got on a Greyhound bus and rode out of the city. I had an idea of what I hoped to find. Outside urban limits, over the bridge and beyond, I expected to see the forests and the rivers and the animals of our country. I had a vision of myself starting someplace new, being someone new, someone real, no more mistakes, I'd get it right this time. I was desperate but hopeful. I thought about who I could be and whom I could be with. I imagined myself healthier, in a green place, everything getting greener all around me. Instead I saw flat fallow fields, tollbooths, beige strips of earth, a toxic highway, punctured houses in the distance, a cellophane horizon, apocalyptic gloom. Gasoline signs hung in the sky. I got down off the bus in a town of grid streets. I walked for miles, turning left at every corner, marking off the territory over and over. I ate my sandwiches and looked at trees drained of leaves, the blue of mailboxes on corners, fossil-logos pressed into the sidewalks, people the shade of cement. A feeling of isolation and doom descended on me. I had no idea what I was doing, I had no plan. Where was I supposed to go? When I'd walked all I could, I went to the Greyhound station and got on the bus heading back to the city because I'd seen there was nowhere to go, nothing out there for me to run to, only straight roads leading to points.

Myers ran. Around him, houses, a tangle of trees, the vile heat. He had trouble focusing his eyes. He tripped, almost fell. He hurried by a line of homes. They were small, made of concrete blocks, with sprays of plant outside, could have Gray inside. He arrived at the end of another meaningless street. Looked each empty way—nothing. Looked behind him. At the other end of the block, a group came around the corner. He could see the dark red slash of the hotel uniform. He ducked into the first place he came to, a walled courtyard.

SPOKE

Three days into conscription, I fled. I escaped over the mountains. I walked. I swam across rivers with my belongings tied to my head. I slept hidden in the bank ferns. I was lost for weeks. One day I saw a pair of Mormons walking across the hills. Once I found a village full of corpses. I arrived in Honduras at last and staggered into town. The soldiers threw a few cold tortillas at me and put me in a camp. Later they sent me to the United States and said, You are in asylum here now. They gave me to a Mexican family and told them to raise me and the family dutifully did. For this reason, when I speak to a Mexican they think I talk almost right but not quite right, and the same with a Nicaraguan. So yes, I am and am not a Nicaraguan, certainly more so than most people are anything and not at once.

Myers stood behind the wall, tugging in air, gulping. Through a barred opening on the other side of the courtyard he could see fallen houses and restaurants, crumbling in the salt air, a discotheque now out of commission, glass-smashed shops. The insane sound of the cicada. He heard footsteps coming up the street, running, maybe two sets, maybe more, he couldn't be sure. He waited. They went by. He was dizzy, needed a steadying, and braced himself against the wall.

THE WIFE'S CONFESSION (PART V)

That might have been the end of it. I might have gone home to my husband, forgotten it, shop-talked and pork-chopped with ease. I got on the bus that stood ready to pull out. I was resolving to myself, my mind revolving. This nice man who loves me and here's how I treat him? I go dashing off, don't even give him a chance to explain? I'm going to do better, I told myself, be better. Something's got to get better and it's going to have to be me. I was saying this to myself. *Better, better, better.*

There was a man in front of me as I boarded the bus. I took no notice at first. A bit of a commotion was going on, people lifting their belongings, trying to fit them into places, people who looked more or less homeless. The man took a seat and as he turned, his face made me think of my husband's. They were the same types—smart young businessmen, vaguely good-looking in the same boyish, blondish way. He had a wedding band on, he looked perfectly normal. Just the sight of him made a little beaker of irritation tip over me because he reminded me of my husband. Then a woman was standing above him.

What are you doing, bozo?

He answered as if startled out of thought, as if lifting the words from my own head, as if he'd been given a dream drug and would now come out with whatever he had in there. I'm leaving, the man said.

I had a sting of understanding.

Good luck, chum, I thought.

The woman said, Not in my seat, you're not.

He fumbled for his coat and headed for the back. He had a sort of skittish, panicked manner to him. There were no more seats nearby and so I also had to continue on toward the back. He took a window seat, the last available window seat. I like window seats. People were behind me and in front. I put down my bag next to him and sat, not because I wanted to, but because there were nearly no seats left and it was time to get out of the aisle. The bus started up. Exhaust filled the air. We sat and waited. I didn't know his troubles and he didn't know mine. We rode that way, side by side, each in our own bewildered state. He stared forward, didn't look out the window, didn't read around in a book. I guess he meant to ride headlong into it, collide if need be, get what was coming, face first. We arrived in New York. The bus drove through a freezing February parade. Streamers clung to the posts and confetti lay strewn in the streets.

I got off the bus. I was curious: was he on his own or would someone come to meet this cheerless creature? I walked behind him out of the station. No one met him. He carried only a black overcoat and a briefcase. He stopped to put on the coat but for nothing else—no phone call, no snack, no restroom visit. He walked out of the station and I got into the taxi line. I watched him go up the street. He was blending in with the other people. In a moment he'd be gone. I stepped out of line to keep him in view a few seconds longer. Where was he going? To a hotel? I wavered. I went after him—not to follow him but just to find out. Where do you go when you leave?

Nowhere, it turned out. He walked east, then south through downtown. He walked under skyscrapers, over bridges. I followed. I didn't have anywhere I had to be. My husband wouldn't be home until the next day and our clean apartment was unnerving. This stranger kept going. The way he walked, it was as if he'd been plopped onto this land from some foreign star and was searching for the way back. Everything about him had a quiet, sad dignity. He spoke to no one that first night. He paused on the bridge to look grimly at the water, then to look up into the sky. The city seemed dinky over there, whiskered with light. Above us, the bridge was a majestic iron prison. The water seemed made of steel. I felt myself moving closer to him, reaching. Then he went on. At last, very late, he came to a brownstone eight blocks from my own. He rang and was let in.

(If things had gone differently for Myers, if he had, say, gone to Corn Island on the afternoon plane, heard the story from Spoke, rejoined his wife eventually, and lived happily ever after, he would have told her Spoke's story and she would have listened and asked questions and been interested.

He had to swim across rivers, Myers would have said. He had to wear his belongings on his head.

Oh, that's very sad, she'd say.

Yes, he'd agree, shaking his head. What our governments do to private citizens in the name of defense...)

Inside the courtyard it was quiet. Myers couldn't leave yet. He'd wait a few minutes to make sure they were gone. He put down the briefcase, leaned into the shade, took deep breaths, bent over coughing. He took inventory, examined his pockets, had a large stack of cash. The damn hospital bill. Like a toy hospital bill, like something you take out for play, that's how little it was—but still, he'd used up the last of his traveler's checks to pay for it. His arm, the unemployed one, was in some sort of wrap, not a cast proper, but a Saran Wrap scenario and it was slack in places, unraveling, the tape coming up, the straight pins loosened in one spot and gripped too tight in another. The entire arm was now aching and the fingers at the end had swelled. There was also the side concern of the ribs. How far did he think he was going to get in this condition?

He had a slip of paper that they'd discharged him with at the hospital, handwritten in English, more helpful advice from his superiors, as if it'd ever done more than get him where he was today.

1. Apply ice
2. Elevate above heart
3. Wiggle uninjured fingers gently and often

SPOKE

So I didn't come back until now, all these years later, until after the war ended, until many years after the war had ended, after we'd all been pardoned by the new government—not the new government after the revolutionary government, but the new government two governments later. We were finally pardoned for running away and they finally sorted it out, who got what and who got nothing and who got invited home. But I didn't come back then either because by then I was a grown man and it hardly mattered anymore and it kept not mattering, but then one day suddenly it did. And here I am, on my vacation, on my first visit home, and one thing I can say about my country is that they sure don't know how to take advantage of the tourist opportunities they have here. They could make a big buck.

Hello, elevate! Unless he wanted to lose the thing!

He propped his arm against the wall.

There may have been things wrong with him from the start, things she'd disliked all along: his unrealized potential, what he hadn't done, what she thought he should have done, his crushing quiet failures, his miniscule moves up the pay scale. Face it, he had been ill-bred, then misled by parents, stifled by teachers who had been shuttled in to represent civilization. Then they waved him out into the disorder alone. Who could want a man like that?

There were also the unmentionables, such as his weaknesses, the stepsister pains of his soul, the sufferings having to do with ego and desire. Not explicable or reasonable, not growing out of the commonplace, but out of the unkempt weeds of the mind.

He saw himself clearly. He had never been happy, not really. She may have known that and hated it.

His arm dropped from the wall. He had to get out of there fast. He saw that clearly too.

THE WIFE'S CONFESSION (PART VI)

I went home. The next morning I woke at dawn. I wasn't going to leave my husband after all, it appeared. A seam of light lay on the sill. I had slept restlessly, had kept walking in my dreams. I felt defeated. I rose. I had only a few more hours of freedom left before the man-and-wife rigmarole resumed. I fiddled with the dishwasher. What would that man do now? I wondered. It doesn't matter, I told myself. I opened the refrigerator—nothing but soda and bread. It occurred to me: The brownstone was right beside the grocery. Maybe a block or two farther. I could go see. Maybe he would give up, get back on the bus, and go home. Or maybe he'd have it in him to stay away. I'd just look. Then get on with things.

I walked back. I hovered outside his brownstone wrapped in my coat, ducked in the shadows, for all the world like a saleswoman selling smack. When he came out, I went after him.

I continued in that manner for four and a half months, as an understudy or a soft-shoe—always a few yards behind. He began a job. I followed him there. Our walks became evening affairs and I had to haul out the long list of lies to my husband, but I barely felt it.

Any other person would have been boring to follow, the same squares drawn on the grid over and over, but this man struck out newly each day. He didn't have the determined stomp of the tourist, more the meandering step of someone tentatively entertaining the thought that he may have lost his way.

I knew this all stemmed at least somewhat from my husband's deceit. I wasn't going to confront him about it. Why should I have to grovel before him to get him to tell me what any husband should tell a wife? I hinted at it, showed him that I knew, to see if he'd break down and confess.

I'm so tired I could drop out the window rather than face the stairs, I'd say.

That woman could go through the glass like a rock, for all I care, I'd say.

No response. He could look as blank-faced as a pie plate. Fine, if that's the way he wanted to play it. I grew angrier and angrier. I kept following the stranger.

I never revealed myself to the man I was following and he never noticed me. It's amazing how unobservant people are, how focused they are on themselves and their own crusades. But it hardly mattered. Between us we had space, silence. We had longing shooting one direction and nothing coming back. His despondency tied me to him. His jagged wanderings. His sad starlight vigils. I gave in to it. I went along.

It was not so different from any relationship, really. I watched but I had no access to his motivations. When he ate, I couldn't tell if he was hungry. When he talked, I didn't know what he said. When he headed home, I didn't know what he found there—I could say the same of my husband. Yes, when he went home he found me there, but what am I?

I recall one day when the man sat down on a bench and I stayed behind a wall so he wouldn't see me. I had to lean over somewhat. I could see the toe of one of his shoes. He had one leg crossed over the other. He bounced it now and then. That's his shoe, I thought. It doesn't matter if the rest of my life is falling apart. I'm taking care of that shoe.

I felt connected to him and who knows that I wasn't? He could be related to me for all I know. He could be my brother. He could have once been my lover during my early crazy days. You never know. We could be married somehow, some mistake could have occurred on the marriage certificate, like a baby being switched at birth—that could have happened—so that during those few months my real husband had been escorting me while the phony stayed at home.

SPOKE

I'll tell you another thing I notice about my country. The chickens sleep in the trees here. I had forgotten that and then I remembered it at my grandmother's. Each evening the chickens follow each other around and around the yard. The head chicken directs. And when the hour of nightfall approaches, they all follow the head chicken up a little staircase into the tree. That's fine with me, everybody's got to have someone in the lead.

There were the expectorants she may have objected to—semen, drool, pus, piss.

Agriculture. Myers wasn't a nature man, if she wanted that.

His autograph, his hair, other components of style. Payday proper as well as investments, potential for growth, sexual habits. She no longer loved him, had not maybe for years, and he would never know why. He didn't want to be alive anymore, didn't care, hadn't cared about anything but her in a long time—and Gray.

The hotel people would coming back this way. He'd better figure out where this Corn Island was and get moving.

Corn Island. Pink-shelled, sandy, spotlit. Myers imagined it: himself, hunchbacked, folded, Gray nearby. But here Myers was, without credit cards, without much cash, down one arm—could he walk there from here? He didn't know which way it was, he didn't know how to get out of this rickety town, how to scoot around the perimeter and avoid the brick-dumb hotel intelligence. He wasn't exactly inconspicuous. But look here, he still had his briefcase and within it the guidebook. A man with a book like that is a man with a place to be.

SPOKE

It's a pretty neat trick the way those chickens go into the tree. My grandmother was working on it when I arrived. She said that the night before somebody had come along and tried to steal one of her chickens. She woke in the night and looked out and saw a man coming down the road under the moon, a dark figure against the pale landscape. He stopped under her tree. Or next to the tree, really. It's a small tree, so the chickens don't have to climb too high. The man stopped and reached in to grab a chicken. But the chicken put up a fuss. He left it and shuffled off.

Myers slid down the wall, propped the guidebook open on his lap.

Getting there was going to be easy street, as they say. It would be what they call a snap. All he had to do, the book said, was first get to a place called Bluefields. It's on the Atlantic coast. What? How was he going to do that? No, no, it was no problem. All he had to do was first find the lake, which was around here somewhere, then get a boat that would take him across it, meanwhile passing four or five more most beautiful islands in the world, according to the guidebook—even though Corn Island was the *most* beautiful, out on a sea, after all, which had to be better than a lake. And, well, he might not be able to get across in one boat, he might have to take a couple, a few—five at most, or six—to get him through that lake. No direct rides. All he had to do was take a boat, then another boat, then another and another, as many as it took, then a bus would take him to a town, then—oh, get this—another boat would take him down a river to Bluefields and from there he didn't know. The guidebook didn't say how to get from the last town to the most beautiful island in the world, and it was a stretch, you could see from the map, a mess of ocean, a hell of a lot of water between the last documented spot and the most beautiful island in the world.

Myers had a question, if you don't mind. Had anyone actually *been* on this island? Were there any *witnesses*?

THE WIFE'S CONFESSION (PART VII)

Of course I couldn't carry on like that forever. Each night I came home and lied to my husband, stood flat-footed through our standoffs, slammed the closest door. I lied to the people at work, shunned friends. I grew more alone and deceitful each day. And it wasn't normal, what I was doing, I knew that. If anyone saw what I was up to, they might call the madhouse. They might call the police. And you know what else? I still wasn't happy, not at all.

The fallout began to fall. I tried to force myself to stop. I made myself go straight home, stare at what I was supposed to, eat what was at hand, but the next day, cursing myself, hating myself, I was back.

Just one more day, I told myself each day, leaving my office early (again), hurrying to his office before he slipped out. That's it now, I swore to myself, arriving home at ten to my indignant husband. That was the last time, I said to myself. But the next day I went on.

Once as I rushed up the street after him, I caught a glimpse of myself in a window. I was wearing a black raincoat and I had an umbrella under my arm. I was scuttling—this is the only way to say it. I was like a cartoon scuttling up the street in a smock. It took me a moment to recognize myself and when I did, I felt drastic, crazy. I hurried on.

SPOKE

The next night she went out to protect her chickens. She waited in the dark for the man to come back. Meanwhile I came walking down the path because it happened to be the same night I was arriving from my foreign land to see my relations for the first time in twenty years. I was swaggering. I was looking at myself. I could see myself—even my shadow was strutting, because I was coming home like a son of the Bible, looking for welcome and ready with my tale. I was imagining them seeing me and the tearful reunion I'd have and how I would later relate it to my child or wife, if I ever had any. I would tell them about that starred night I showed up at my grandmother's many years after I'd left and gone to a country where my words grew confused and I forgot what was home and never remembered again. I came walking down the path in the dark and I could see my grandmother's lean form outside.

She came into the path, pointed a mop.

Stop right there, she said. Don't think I don't know who you are.

No, no, there will be transport, the guidebook assured. He just had to show up in Bluefields and say, Where's this Corn Island, the most beautiful island anyone ever heard of? I could use something like that just now, I really could.

Which Corn Island do you want? they would say.

Which! For crying out loud. There's more than one of the damn things?

All right, yes, the guidebook admitted. There are two. But Myers wanted the bigger one, of course, because what is better—a bigger most beautiful island or a smaller?

THE WIFE'S CONFESSION (PART VIII)

I knew from the beginning that anyone who could leave a home as evenly as he had could leave a new home too. He could disappear the same way he had come, and that would be the end of it. It was likely to happen no matter what I did.

I began to dread it. I wasn't sure I could bear it if he left. I decided I would leave when he did. I'd step out of this wrong life I had made and into a new one. I'd follow him right out of town. I figured I would have some indication, some warning of his intention, a suitcase in his hand perhaps, but if not, it didn't matter. I was determined not to lose him. At that point I was following him with the persistence and intensity of the noonday sun. And I could go on forever this way. But I knew, even as I formulated this plan, that it was ridiculous, absurd. I didn't care. I bid farewell to my husband in my head. I kept some gum in my purse for the ride.

People do things like this, they *do*, and if it doesn't make them happy, at least it keeps them alive.

One day I followed him into the bus terminal.

Myers looked up from the guidebook. What was that noise? Were they coming back? He listened. Not yet, but it was time to make his move.

He wasn't going to be able to lug much. He'd lost most of it already. The hotel personnel left to hold down the hotel were probably this minute going through his suitcase. He didn't need all those belongings anyway, all those coats and whatever he had there, a suit for God's sake, and that hat, all that cloth carried over land and water. Still, he hated the idea of their opening the suitcase, shaking out the winter coat, holding it up in confusion. Was there something wrong with this fellow (tap to the forehead) upstairs? Is it any wonder he didn't pay his bill?

SPOKE

So my reunion turned out to be awkward, what with my being almost attacked with a stick and run off the land like a goat. Then my relations thought I spoke funny, though they tried to be polite. They all had the same question. They all wanted to know, if I loved them so much, why hadn't I come back sooner? All the other boys had come back years ago.

What took *you* so goddamn long to come home? they said.

THE WIFE'S CONFESSION (PART IX)

He went into the bus station, bought a ticket. I didn't want to lose him in line so I would buy mine on board. I waited for him outside the men's room, then wandered behind while he strolled to the gate. My hands were shaking. My vision was blurred. I followed him up to the last moment but when he set his foot on the bottom step of the bus, I fell back. I watched him go. The bus pulled away. Who knows why he went.

I remained.

Because that, it turns out, is who I am.

I lack the courage it takes to go after whatever disastrous thing it is that I want and the fortitude to accept gracefully the bad choices I've made. Leaving, staying, it's all too hard. I'm still walking around these same places. I am itinerant but steadfast. It takes bravery to care for someone—no matter who he is or what made him, whether he is weak or walking or jumping out of windows. The risk involved is enormous.

As for him, the fact is he had gotten on the same bus he had come in on. Maybe everyone goes back. We chase the thing we flee.

After he left, I don't want to say I moved like a shadow over the face of the earth or be as dramatic or as religious as that, though it was like that. I was still married, it turned out. I was practically not married, that's how new it was, and if anyone tells you it's easy to fake love, well, let me tell you, you cannot know the emptiness of my world those first few months. The city was nothing but an enormous unfolded newspaper. And there was this husband that needed caring for and a job to be gone to and got from. There was the purchase of objects and the consuming of them. One can watch the screen to feel numb.

Most people have about as much as that, I think, although I could be wrong. I don't pay gobs of attention.

What did Myers even need from this briefcase? He didn't need the laptop anymore with the precious projects on it, just electronic stains and punctuation marks, a black-smudged screen. A man needed to be covered up, of course, and he seemed to be that. Jelled items having to do with cleanliness and presentation, especially around the face and mouth, would be useful, and a few other small things he had here.

He put the laptop on the ground.

SPOKE

The next day my grandmother decided she needed a taller tree to keep the chickens safe, so she built a new staircase going up a taller tree, and she dismantled the old staircase leading to the shorter tree. But at sunset she couldn't get the head chicken to go into the new tree. The chicken stood by the old one squawking. This isn't surprising. Nobody knows a new home. My grandmother took a broom and chased the chickens around with it while I watched from the porch. She raised masses of dust. Finally the head chicken found the new staircase, mounted it, first one step, then another. The chicken looked around. She went up a third step. She called to the others, and one by one they all followed her up into the new tree.

Ahoy, Myers,

I'm waiting. Did you come yesterday? I thought I saw you but you left too fast for me to step on your tail and hold you here. I can't find the airport here in paradise. I can't find the exit ramp, the elevator down. There seems to be no trapdoor, no fire escape, no knob to rattle. Come get me. I'm ready. I want to go home.

Gray

So with only briefcase, his other final belongings gone (he'd never miss his coats, the raincoat, he'd always despised it, and the heavy wool one, he'd always despised it too, and the suitcase, so what, papers, a pile of clothing) (Myers looked out the gate, the street was unpeopled both ways)—

So with briefcase and that much decided, he walked over the last of the earthquake, continued on into the impeding day.

Somewhere around now his injured arm began to throb.

THE WIFE'S CONFESSION (PART X)

If I thought of us as prophets, there in the city, each with our own message quiet in our throats, which of us was the one hearing the message for the first time, gathering it for future broadcast, coming to terms with its calling? And which of us was the outcast, shunned, without followers, thought mad for our strange predictions? And which of us was the retired prophet—message delivered, prophecy fulfilled, sinners punished—now sliding through the hubbub, breaking away, exiting, heading home, his business here done?

Myers turned left and headed for the lake. Above, a queer light, a bluing landscape.

THE WIFE'S CONFESSION (PART XI, CONCLUSION)

I don't want to talk about my husband. I will say only that I did not mean to behave uncivilly. But who ever found themselves married to a man who jumped out a window? Yes, I should have asked him why he did it and why he hid it. Don't ask me about him. Please don't say another word. Don't ask me anything at all. I despise a querying man. You have a question? Bring it to your accountant.

I think I can be comfortable with you thinking the worst of me.

That is all I have to say.

End of confession.

Chapter Fifteen

RECEPTIONIST

She was hanging around the embassy all day—the man's ex-wife, yes. It wasn't my business and I wasn't going to make it so. The people in the office were ignoring her, of course. She had her baby with her, a little girl about three or four years old. The girl was well-behaved, better behaved than the woman anyway, who sat there looking hysterical all day and every now and then got up and came over to me and acted hysterical and talked about her husband and some emails he'd sent her and then sometimes she got as far as the office and I could hear her in there acting hysterical too. But mostly she sat in the waiting room with a piece of Kleenex in her hand that she pressed to her eyes or held in her fist. She waited a long time. I wanted to tell her, Don't feel so bad. Nobody cares about me and my problems either.

I had my own ugly project that day. I was using a pen that I hated. It was a cheap ballpoint and it kept leaking all over the page. Globs and smears of black ink. God, I hate this pen, I kept thinking. The pen was just like my husband, who'd left me the week before. The pen was like everything I dislike about him—messy, cheap, broken—and it was for that very reason, because the thing reminded me of him and because it was in fact his, one of the cheap broken items he'd left behind, that I was determined to write with it to the bitter end, until it went dry, no matter the mess. He had never loved me, he'd said. Let the ink bleed.

So I was working on that, filling in forms with smudges and blots, and this tearful woman was sitting there all day, calling people on her cellphone and telling me the story again and again, about how her husband was missing. Line up, lady!

It was the girl who finally did it for me. While her mother was making a nuisance, the girl sat, swinging her legs, looking around. She hopped off her seat, stepped across to my desk, where I was furiously scratching away with my pen. She put her little hand up, peeked over the edge of the desk.

Yes? I snapped. Yes? Yes?

We can't find my daddy, she said.

I put down the pen at last. Where did you lose him?

I couldn't do much more than get the U.S. Embassy in Managua to send their people out, to alert whomever they had wherever they were to keep an eye out. A man with a massive brain tumor, of all things, who would be showing other symptoms by now, physical and social.

Chapter Sixteen

All right, yes, once Myers went out a window. Nearly any moron could manage it. He was twelve years old and chasing a bird that had flown in, sailed around the apartment, and then out, Myers following. The bird unreeled into the sky, swept over the heartsick city and rose. Myers leapt after that bird as if attached by a rope, as if chaperoned or prodded with a stick. He dropped five stories and landed on his head, the remainder of his body heaped behind. His skull cracked into thirty-one pieces, made a cushion for his brain to sink into. He spent eleven weeks in the hospital, five in a coma and six coming out. In the end he rose up out of the bed like Jesus and walked away (first hobbling through rehab, then tossing away his stick like a new believer). He continued his life without alteration, dully. No one except him could have detected any difference. The before and after, those parts of it were equal.

The first image he saw with precision as he came out of the coma was the bottom half of a water vase on the bedstand. Then the mess behind it, the apples or chocolates or wrappings piled up—what *was* all that crap?

Items shrank and enlarged in his eye that morning. The nurse's uniform, his father's brown, the geometry of the ceiling tiles (sensation: of falling), a few robotish structures set to one side, a small knickknack stuffed and giraffe-looking that had dropped off under a chair. And so on.

No memory loss for him. He was utterly, vaguely aware. The soaring bird, the leap, the fall, he could see it all, carbon-star dark.

What it's like to be in a coma: How should he know? He wasn't there for it. He later wondered where he'd been stored in the meantime, the weeks of it, of functioning only on backup power and emergency lights while the rest of him, most of him, floated out in the dark in a lifeboat. On waking, he had no new understanding, made no resolutions, signed no new leases, saw no visions of the perfect world to come.

The doctors stitched the parts back together to form a rocky whole. At home Myers turned side to side in the mirror and considered. He couldn't detect any bumps or swells, but the thoughts themselves seemed to be chipped or chinked, like seeing through water, so objects appear bent or of unnatural lengths. He felt that way and he felt that one of the holes hadn't sealed up completely, that it gaped still. He walked to the corner store in the cold and he could feel the wind blow through it and freeze his brain, freeze his thoughts even. He also felt like things were falling out of it, like a heavy shake might dent it further. He could sometimes feel the half-healed lines left behind on his skull, he could sense them, he could run his fingers over them.

Does it show? he asked his father.

His father looked at his mother.

Nope, not at all, she said. Looks good.

His family moved across town. He left home and moved across

another town. Soon he saw no one who had known him on both sides of the accident. Soon no one he knew knew.

Puzzlehead. Soft skull. These and other descriptions occurred to him. He didn't tell her. Not before the wedding or after. He felt inarticulate. Foolish. Defensive. He wasn't a realist. Had no interest in an objective statement of his life. She couldn't tell so why should he?

It never occurred to him that she knew. He was so accustomed to behaving as if it'd never happened that neither her hints nor anyone else's broke through the insulation and sheetrock of his consciousness. Maybe he didn't want them to. Maybe he preferred not to know that the incident, so large a part of his dim internal world, lit up so brightly on the surface.

My dearest wife,

I don't know why you would report the credit cards stolen unless you wanted me out of the way for good. I suppose I was wrong in assuming you would at the very least extend to me the courtesies any individual deserves who has the foresight to obtain a wife—the whole point of marriage being the guarantee that there exists one citizen on earth who is under contract to deal honestly with you.

As it stands you are under breach of contract. You are against the law.

That being the case, I will take this opportunity to tell you that I know you followed that guy, for months and months and months. You trailed him instead of me. That was the initial betrayal done in the dawn of our marriage and this is the furthering of that. There, I have said it: I know.

In Granada, it turned out, a boat left the lakeshore twice a day and everybody walked up a ramp to get on. Lucky for Myers (the one moment of luck he seemed to have—too bad it couldn't have been a bigger one, longer, farther reaching) he arrived just as the ramp was being pulled back and all he had to do was give a shout and run up. The ramp was a thin strip of rotted wood suspended over the water and Myers had to decide to be brave, had to determine not to have an existential crisis in crossing it. He did and he did. He was brave, there was no crisis, his feet held the steady tread of a man who had done this all his life. He was on.

A few half-dead fish washed up onshore, vines lined down the sand, parrots rising in clusters. Far off, he saw three men in hotel livery running down the shore, arms in the air, waving. They were small, still had a distance to go.

The boat coasted off.

My husband,

I don't know how you could have known my movements without having me followed or without following me yourself, which I consider to be your own breach of contract, the alleged pledge of allegiance between husband and wife, the part about trust and free will, the nondetermination clause, the criminal trespassing clause, the anti-martial marital law clause. I cannot find the fine print just now but there must be a clause in the wedding contract that stipulates the allowance of certain freedoms, such as movement, such as sight, the freedom to look in one direction as opposed to another. Unless you stapled an unfriendly amendment onto the original, which I know very well you did not.

In any case, you can prove nothing. I did nothing. I admit to nothing and feel the guilt of a sparrow or of any lifting bird. It is a basic tenet of those who agree to live in democratic states, that is, in a state of being that accepts concepts such as rights, citizenship, and so on, that a person be allowed to walk down a city block if she likes and to walk back up it if she reaches the end and is unsatisfied or if for some other reason, undisclosed even to her own heart, she chooses to turn and walk back. And I have so chosen. I have so on many occasions, as many as I have decided not to, and I will not explain these choices. I will not.

Your devoted wife

He got off at the first stop to throw off his pursuers—in case they decided to jump into the lake after him. He managed to get on a boat full of priests. They had to make room for him among their books and rods and their holy baggage.

The next boat he got on was a business boat, carrying nothing but sand and rocks. They were bringing the shipment to the Atlantic, they said, for export to Haiti. They carried it over the lake, then through the sea from the docks.

The sand part made sense to him, but why bring rocks?

Sand of the future, they said, which Myers thought odd because surely they had rocks on Haiti.

No, the rocks had all been smashed to bits and carted away. At Navidad, they said, this same boat exports leafage to the north. Sad fact, what happens to the northern leaves each year. If he came back then, he'd take his own fistful home free.

My dearest wife,

Say what you like, I will not force your word. I know you followed Gray. He carried a briefcase. He was stooped. Or sometimes he stood up straight. I followed him too and I do still today though I do not care to, though it broke my heart and my limbs. Admit nothing, but can you tell me this: If you were to follow such a man, what would your reason be? Would you do it because you loved him?

He rode on a knife-selling boat. The walls of the boat were made up of strips of differently sized plywood, not quite cardboard, not quite wood, each a square foot or two and painted bright colors, fitted irregularly and nailed together like a jigsaw.

Seems like you have the mug of a wanted man, said the knife man, sharpening his ware.

Sure do, said Myers. In want of a drink.

Police boat came by, the knife man said, squinting out at the horizon. Talked about a man who matches your description.

Not me, said Myers. I look like anyone. This lake is full of people who look like this.

You headed to Corn Island?

(Damn Spoke. He must have told them.)

Haiti, said Myers.

You one of those Haitian boat people?

What do I look like?

So what are you doing in this lake?

My loving husband,

What can you mean that you follow him too? All I know is that like all people who try to justify their stand, you do what you want to do and then you say your way is right. You exaggerate the morality of your position and the immorality of mine. If I were to follow such a man, I couldn't tell you why because you wouldn't understand. But I can tell you that any man who lied to me, who kept vital information secret, would not receive my admiration.

Your gentle wife

And his briefcase got soaked, of course, as did his leather shoes, his pant cuffs, his seat. Well, what was he going to do about it. You can't protect everything. Water, mud, earth. Eventually everything returns to the same color.

My dearest wife,
Lie? What lie?

The lie about your head.

I never told you anything about my head.

Hello? I never told you anything about my head.

About the time you jumped out the window. You never told me.

Fell. I fell out the window.

Jumped. You jumped. There were witnesses.

I fell.

All right, let's say "went." The time you went out the window.

Each time he toppled out onto a dim brackish shore, he got on the next boat, and the next, and the next. Who could have known a lake could be so large and contain so much in it? But he couldn't stop to rest. He got up and sat down when people pointed and told him to and he picked up his briefcase when it was in the way. He moved from island to island across the lake, each spot winging him a little farther from one side and a little closer to the other.

Gray, Nicaragua is driving me crazy. I'd do anything to make it out of here. The woman I love is far away and the town I've stopped in sells only a gross drink called Rojita. I'm almost out of money and I've got the police after me now. My ribs are cracked. My arm is broken. My fingers have numbed. Look, can we meet someplace else? Corn Island is a bit tricky just now. How about San Juan del Sur? Five-dollar lobster, turtle days, two for one, southern sun, Peace Corps singalongs. What do you say?
    Myers

Myers! Get up on those legbones and hobble over here. I'm in some kind of overgrown maze, enemy planes above. But you can get in on the highway and lead me out—bring the binoculars.
    Gray

Okay, Gray, Corn Island it is. I can see San Juan is out. I'll get there somehow, but be ready to make a run for it. Get out your best sunhat, pocket the lotion. Stay where you are. I'm coming to get you.

Myers staggered up the shore. He was so worn out, he wanted to lie down in the water. He made it over to the men. I'm looking for a boat, he said.

Looks like we're looking for you, one said.

How's that?

You fit the description, more or less.

Goddamn it—Myers must have really been a slowpoke to move so slowly across this country and to so slowly register just how far these hotel people were willing to go for their few hundred bucks. They would enlist boat police, boy scouts, strangers from far-off lands. They'd send out a fleet to float through a mosaic of islands. Myers stood there awhile, considering running, though these guys looked pretty tough, and where was he going to run? He was so tired.

Fine, Myers said at last. Toot the horn. Whistle the dogs. I give up. I'm done.

About time, they said. What a fuss you've made.

What's going to happen to me?

You tell us, buddy. We don't know what you've done.

I don't care. Just take me in.

Take you? they said. Are we a taxiboat? A busboat? You go yourself.

Where?

For God's sake, man, you go by the name Gray?

Gray? Myers said.

Your wife wants you home, one said, crooking a finger at him.

My wife?

Better get moving, he said. You know how the ladies are.

All right, Myers said, carefully.

On the double, buddy. That way's the boats.

All right, Myers said again. He limped off.

160

My dearest wife,

All right, I'll tell you from the beginning but it won't change anything now. It began long before our marriage, long before I ever held your hand. It began on a day not unlike this one. Warm, sunny, clear. I was following a bird and the next thing I knew I was out the window. I suppose there was agency in it, yes. I could have stopped at the ledge but I didn't. I chose not to. So what? It's what I did and in some way it makes me who I am. I am the man who went out the window, dropped five stories, and landed on his head. I didn't intend it or see it coming. That is, I didn't see the pavement coming up fast. I do recall the framed sky, a bird sliding through a slot in it, my hand reaching as I approached the window. The outside was nothing but posterboard. Then the foothold, the tailspin, and my head crushed like a cantaloupe.

Sometimes we act without reason. Sometimes we have only the dim conviction that we have expressed ourselves vividly.

Since that fall, I have felt apart from others. Misaligned. As if somehow that contact with cement knocked me off course, steered me astray. I have lived a half-life, a papery existence. Except in my best days with you, I have felt morbidly alone and uncertain. I can't say I wish I had died because I'm not certain I'm not dead. I can't say I wish I had lived because I seem to be alive. I feel a little more dead than yesterday though, a little less alive. Today I'm on my way to Corn Island. I have only the vaguest idea of where it might be and the name itself means nothing. But I have one more thing to take care of.

Your adoring husband

THE WIFE'S CONFESSION (APPENDIX)

I gave him a rock once. I dug it out of the sand with a stick and wiped the dirt off with my thumbs. We were at the beach, just married. It was our honeymoon. We hardly knew each other back then—I'd like to know how many people look at their spouses and think that. I'd bet quite a few.

What's this, a rock? he said. What's so neat about that?

He put it on the towel, had his crossword back in his hand.

No one's ever touched it before, I said. Except me. And now you.

He picked it up again. It had a glint in it like an emerald.

It does seem ridiculous but what I meant was that no one had ever touched *me* before. I didn't want to have to say it and I knew with him I didn't have to say it. He knew my heart was a rock and that was okay with him. That was something about him: in some deep way and despite all else wrong with him, with us, he accepted me.

He kept the rock. It's still here.

MARIA

Did he fall out of bed or did he just climb onto the floor? I came for the light and he was on the floor, the sheet with him, tangled. If he was going to fall on the floor, I wasn't going to be able to watch every minute and make sure he didn't and I told him so. After that he stayed in the bed. Only once he got up and tried to walk around the room. Four days ago was the last time he went out by himself. He went to the Internet café two doors down and had to be helped back. He won't be doing it again.

He's dying, that's all. I'm just watching.

I've been the owner of the hotel since my husband left eight years, seven months ago.

Yesterday I called my neighbor because she was once a dancer in the U.S., will never stop talking about it and how she speaks English and had such beautiful legs and how all the men of Miami sent her blooms. So she came over to be an interpreter. We went up to his room and stood over him in the bed. What do you want me to say? she said.

I said, Ask him does he know he's sick.

She did and he said, Yes, by force if necessary.

Okay, I said, ask him does he want some soup.

Of course he wants soup, she said. Look at him, he always wants soup.

Ask him does he know where he is, I said.

So she did and he lay there thinking. He clearly didn't know.

Okay, ask him if he's in an airport, a hotel, or at home.

He thought about it and then said airport, which, okay, because there was a rumbling noise out the window that was a truck but could have been a plane.

Ask him where he's going, I said.

Don't play him for dumb.

Ask him does he know why he's here. Ask him what he wants us to do. Does he know he's dying? Ask him that. Does he want to live?

Leave the poor man alone, my neighbor said. She's bringing you soup, she said to him.

We went downstairs to the kitchen and we said together, Oh my God, can you believe how messed that man is in the head as well as the body? He is doomed, we said, doomed, doomed.

Today he is worse and I know it because his eyes are glossy and his breath is coming in gasps and I know it will not be long. I call the doctor over and he says days now. Is his family coming? he wants to know

Family? I say. Am I supposed to find his family?

Write a letter to the U.S. Embassy, woman.

So I write the letter and I mean to post it but it's too late, the next day he dies.

Chapter Seventeen

Myers had already had it by the time he took his life jacket and sat where he was told. But he knew by the map that he didn't have much farther to go. Then the man said they were short two people and without them they couldn't go on.

The man said they would wait. So they sat, jammed in and lined in rows, low in the muddy water, the jungle around them darkening by degrees. Maybe they sat for two hours. At last people began to stand, pull their life jackets over their heads, climb out of the panga.

Where are you going? Myers said.

Someone will come, he said.

But no. No one was coming. The hot wind blew. They would all reassemble in the morning at five and try again.

In the morning he and the others reassembled in the panga. Someone else had arrived in the night on a boat, or a bus, or a horse, or a cart. Now there was one space left and they sat in their life jackets waiting. The sun was an unfriendly arrow. Finally three people came walking down the dock with their boxes and nets and suitcases. To Bluefields? they said. Bluefields?

Nobody knew what to do.

At last they had to admit they were going there too. And everyone took off their life jackets and climbed out of the panga, one by one, and walked across the dock to a bigger panga and put on other life jackets and sat back down. Everything was fine. Until the man who owned the first panga came walking over in a slouch.

It was all right with him. His feelings weren't hurt. He didn't mind if they wanted to take the other man's panga. Even if he had bought the gas. Even if he had sat with them for hours one day and hours another. He didn't mind. But no way was anybody getting their money back.

Myers wanted to say, For God's sake, let's just all pay again, but even he needed his cash.

So they all took off their life jackets and lined off the bigger panga and got back on the smaller panga and put back on the other life jackets and sat back down. Somehow they managed to squeeze all three of those men on too.

And then the owner said, We can't go on, the boat is sinking. And indeed it was, water spilling over the sides. So two of the three men climbed out of the panga and stood on the dock with their luggage in a pile beside them. The town spired behind them. And then the panga was off.

They told Myers to sit in the middle. Get in the middle, they said, but he wouldn't budge. He wanted to look at the jungle as they passed or some such thing, some remnant of "vacation" torn off and left hanging in his mind. But as soon as they started going he could see why they said to get in the middle. The water lifted like a wall and sprayed into the boat, and then it began to rain and everybody at once pulled a giant piece of plastic over the boat, which the people not in the middle had to hold down with their fingers. Which with an arm in a sling it was very hard to hold. Myers's side kept flying up and everyone yelled at him and finally they made him crawl over someone and get in the middle like they'd said in the first place.

Then the luggage flew off the boat and into the water. Huge boxes, which broke when they hit the surface, and clothes went everywhere. Rain poured out of the sky like in the days of Noah, but they had to pull off the plastic and go back and the people not in the middle had to lean over into the water and fish the clothes out of the river and put them, wet-heavy, in the boat between their legs.

In truth, here is the story: A man leaves a place. A man leaves another place. And another. And another. He has to keep leaving and sometimes it is good and sometimes it is not, but mostly not. It is just a series of departures, of doors closing, a briefcase snapping shut. Nothing becomes clearer. Nobody changes. The man wants to change but cannot. The man wants to change the woman he loves and left but cannot do that either, stubborn stuck nails that humans are—failure of evolution or God. The man makes plans in any case. Between boats. He writes them out longhand, crumbles them up, writes them again, more carefully this time or in a different size lettering: The New Plan. Or: The Old Plan Revised. Or: Revised New Plan. Or: Second Revision of Second Plan. The plans are all the same. They all involve resolutions to quit certain habits (her, there, then), to resign himself to different ones (here, this, that), and then to commit himself to those habits of resignation, not to falter but to carry on, be resigned in the following ways, be the person those habits make one become regardless of former resolutions or habits, regardless of which sunny road it may lead away from. Each plan is based on one overarching resolution, the essential one, the one without which he can do nothing else, or he can but it won't work because the first part must be in place before anything else can follow,

anything other than humiliation, frustration, pain, and maybe prison: Leave. Leave this place now.

This is what it came down to. He said that in his mind: This is what it's come down to, what I've come up with, what I've come to. We all, he said, must shift our position immediately or else go down further still.

Does anybody have a boat? said Myers.

I'll pay anyone with a boat, he said.

This was on the next island.

Come with me, said a boy. They walked on planks of wood thrown across the mud. They stood on a porch and called into the dark, ¿Disculpe, hay barco? A woman in shadows shook her head sadly, No, no hay barco. They went everywhere—to the school, which was closed, to the office of stamps, to another office whose light swung in and out in the distance. The escort introduced him grandly. He is going to Bluefields. He must get out of this lake. His mother is sick. His wife worried. His boss apoplectic. The escort spoke long and eloquently. He used his hands to express the wife's desire, the American's duty, the escort's efficiency. They walked back on a road as blue as Bluefields in dreams.

On the next island (he was almost there now), Myers would have to go to the other side to catch a boat, they said. He'd have to walk around. No, no, not cut through the grass like a fool (Myers was no fool), what did he want, a good old snakebite in those grasses? He'd be dead before he was found.

But he couldn't walk all the way around, he said. It looked long, it looked far. He had an arm that was first broken, then patched, then hurting, now wet. And his side was sore too.

It really isn't far, they said. But, okay, where's Nico?

Where's Nico? they said.

Nico careened over with his crazy limp, a man shining with youth. He took Myers's briefcase and put it in a shopping cart. He put Myers in

168

the shopping cart. He wheeled him away. The town lined up to watch as they bumped down the rock road. Everyone cheered.

The boat on the other side was six dollars and Myers had to bail one-handed with a tin cup the water that collected at the bottom, but it wasn't too bad as far as these things go. No sinking went on.

And he finally did arrive.

And Gray? What about him?

Never made it to Nicaragua. He stayed on in David, Panama, a town so hot the fruit in the carts melted into wax and the large sheets of *loteria* that should flutter stayed pasted to the boards with wood sweat. A cool breeze ran through the dreams of citizens but never through the trees. The only tourist trinkets sold were the *molas* the Indians stitched and hung from the trees, but no one did that in this town because there were no tourists. Gray stayed. He slept in room 433 of the Hotel Central on the plaza for twelve dollars a night. He woke each morning and went to the café. He ate two eggs at the counter alongside the other men of the town. Then he walked to the iron benches under the trees in the plaza—the one place in town that offered respite from the heat—until sunset when the birds whipped up a frenzy and screamed across the sky. He ate chicken with *pejibaye* folded into a paper cone from a blistering streetside grill. He visited the Internet café on the corner, went back to his room. The people of the town accepted him, assumed he was one of the gringos left behind from the days when the U.S. controlled the canal. As his actions grew slower and his responses more erratic, they figured he'd been abandoned here, deserted like a sick animal or like a battered piece of machinery that could no longer be of use. There was plenty of that here, left by the U.S., further demonstration of the hard-hearted, handy mind of the North American.

He wrote home less and less, read his emails without comprehension, the frantic messages from his ex-wife, and when he wrote back he spoke of their coming to visit rather than his going home. He never left the town again, although as his dementia increased he believed he did. Once he woke thinking he'd ridden a sleeper car though the night and had arrived in a new place. Once he believed that in an ambling walk he'd gone straight to a new town, made new friends, settled in. And yes, he resolved to go to Corn Island after reading its entry in the guidebook. He never thought he'd arrived, but he believed he was on his way and urged his ex-wife, daughter, and Myers to join him. In this way his life seemed dull but his brain was not. After a time he couldn't walk anymore, beyond a slow toddle to the corner and back, and after a time more, not even that. The owner of the hotel brought soup to him twice a day, stopped charging him rent. It was she who closed his eyes when he died. She sent the letter to the embassy but received no response. She ran an obituary in the English-language newspaper and she added what she correctly assumed to be true: Mr. Gray chose our country for his first and last voyage from home.

This was as far as the owner or anyone else went in searching for his relations. The ex-wife and daughter never learned of his death.

So Myers was finally in Bluefields. And now the question was: why Bluefields? He couldn't recall. Certainly he must have had a reason to propel him forward each dawn. If not an original reason that he'd forgotten, at least a purported reason, one he told people over and over, one he emailed home. It couldn't be that he thought he would find tourists at the other end. Bank machines and beaches and blue skies and song. Bring on the Caribbean dream. He couldn't have thought that. Who other than he would come this far and go this long? Who other than he? He walked from the dock, numb-wet, wanting only the Internet. The main street was a pit of mud.

No, no, it's not Bluefields itself that he wants. It's the other one, Corn Island.

What is that?

Remember? It's the island. The beach, the song, the sky.

What does he want with that?

170

Gray.

Oh, yes.

Also.

Yes?

The wife. She likes a beach.

Oh, for God's sake.

At that point it seemed impossible that he could still be looking for the man his wife followed or be waiting for his wife to arrive, but he was. Maybe it was a different man or a different wife or maybe the same ones with different names. Maybe there was no wife anymore, only the habit of emails home. He took a room in the Hotel Caribbean Dream, of all things, for four dollars a night. He was the only guest.

That day in Bluefields, he didn't see any tourists like he hoped. A truck like a tank wobbled down the street and sprinkled a great mist of repellant over them all. The earth rumbled with a minor quake and everyone held out their hands for balance. But then he came back to his hotel and saw a North American sitting on a step as if they were in Brooklyn.

I haven't seen anyone like me in a week, said Myers.

A week? he said. Who's like you? There's no part of that sentence I understand.

Where are the tourists, said Myers, the reggae bars?

I've never seen a tourist here. He studied Myers. Is that what you are?

No, I'm just here to check my email.

And lo and behold he and Myers were from the same town although the man didn't know how to act like someone from that town anymore. He kept speaking the wrong language.

In the U.S. we speak English these days, Myers thought it fair to inform him.

Is that right? And what was I speaking?

I don't know what that was.

And lo and behold the man knew just where Myers could check his email. As they walked through the streets to reach it, the man said, I can get you a girlfriend, a local, just so you know.

I have a wife, Myers said. (He wasn't sure of that.)

That's an angry arm you got there.

It's a little crunched.

You looked banged up elsewhere too. You get in a fight?

I could use a doctor, Myers admitted.

Oh yeah, a doctor. Just be careful. Don't let anyone do any voodoo on you.

Myers had no new messages.

It was on a hill they walked up that he told Myers what had happened, how he'd got stuck in this spot. They walked up that hill in the heat and drizzle for the same reason people ride rivers or sail out into the sea.

I was fishing off the coast of Bluefields, the man said. I had a crew of three. I was standing on the deck, looking out at the water. Suddenly they jumped on me, three at once, and hit me over the head with a pipe.

A pirate ship! said Myers.

Not a pirate ship, he said, a little annoyed. It was my fishing ship, my crew.

They jumped on me, he said. One was hitting my legs with the pipe and another was hitting my head. Blood everywhere. I wouldn't go down.

Why not? Myers gasped.

I was screaming, I was crazy. I don't know what I was doing. I went down at last. They tied me up with cord. Look, I have scars still. Look at my ankles. Still I limp from the pipe.

He still had scars around his ankles, thick, uneven rings.

They held a machete to my throat, he said. You're going to fucking die, man, die in Bluefields, one kept saying.

Let me do him right now, another kept saying. Then they locked me in a room and left me there. I pushed the air conditioner out the window and jumped into the water. I escaped.

Factors in viewing from above a man going overboard into a temptuous sea: how far away the viewer is from the scene, what the light is like, what color the water is.

Imagine a particular case. The water and sky are the same storm shade. And the man himself is quite colorless. His clothes wet, muddy. The boat is leaden, and there are people on it and an animal on it. The light is dim through the clouds. Rain darkens the scene further. From very high up, anyone looking down would see only a shifting of various shades of the same hue, as the waves roll and toss the boat. The boat itself appears as an ink mark on the graywash. At most, one might see something coming off it, flying out across the waves, a narrow piece a shade lighter than the other colors, visible only for a moment before disappearing. A few minutes later, one might see a second piece, slightly smaller, detach from the boat.

Or if viewed from a little closer, the ink mark might resolve into some sort of military boat, the first slice into a figure. Closer, and one might see that the first is a man and the second is an animal, both flying into the sea.

It was freezing in that water, he told Myers. And shark-infested. I was bleeding. I was so far from land. I swam for hours. At last I made it and crawled up on the rocks. I ran to a door, a long trail of blood behind me. I pounded on the door and an old man opened it. I told him, I'll give you five hundred dollars cash. I'll go to the bank and give you five hundred dollars cash if you'll drive me in your boat to the U.S. military base right now.

You said that? Myers gasped.

Well, first I asked him for a glass of water. I was immensely thirsty. Can I have a glass of water? I said, and then I said I'd give him five hundred bucks. The old man said, Five hundred U.S. dollars? All right, let's go! And we went out to his boat but the damn thing wouldn't start. He kept trying and finally I said, Old man, give me that thing, and I nearly tore the engine off.

Myers had never heard of anybody going through something like that and not going home.

What happened to the engine? he asked.

I started it and I was saved.

In Bluefields it was dusk and a hundred years' worth of birds were flying in, coming over the rooftops. The birds landed and landed on wires, on posts. Still more arrived and more, circling in from all sides. They were strikes, clouds. The noise was an invasion, the air was a long note. It cannot be described on a page. It would be impossible to capture in a movie. There is no way to represent it. Being there wouldn't do it. You'd have to *be Myers*, see what he saw. It was like an emergency, like he had stopped breathing, the first bell toll of the apocalypse. Meanwhile around them men chopped their coconut, chatted among themselves. That's simply how things move in this wet country.

I'd like to go home, the man said. Are you like most people at home?

Myers is like most people at home.

Chapter Eighteen

What is your wife doing right now?

Is it depressing not to know? What kind of life did she want that you weren't able to give her? What part of your life did she reject? That is, what part of *you* did she reject?

Did she want money? Did she want youth? Did she want fun? Did she want someone else, someone new, someone without the same problems, opinions, body as yours? Let me ask you this: Do you know, do you have any idea what she wanted? Do you have any idea what went wrong?

Do you have any idea how *you* went wrong?

If she were able to name something specific that was wrong with you—not enough money, say—would that help at all? Would that just be another way to keep you at a distance under pretense?

Do you think another man could offer her something you couldn't? Did she think so? What would it be? Why didn't you ask her? What were you afraid of? Have you ever asked her what she thinks about?

Have you ever asked her anything at all?

Why did you stop being nice to her?

When did you stop making love to her?

If it's true that she knew you'd be stuck out of the country, don't you find that disturbing? Is it possible she'd been planning this all along?

She could be lifting a dish, she could be soaping her hair, she could be riding the train, brewing a cup of tea, putting down a magazine, packaging up your belongings, folding clothing into a bag, fucking or following another man. What do you think she's doing, if anything? What do you think she's thinking about, if anything? What do you think she thought about when she followed Gray up the street, down to the train? Not you, certainly, but what? Does it bother you not to know?

Let's say she's walking toward Gray right now. Let's say he's with her. Let's say he's not in Central America at all.

How do you feel about that?

Did it actually surprise you to lose your job?

Did it actually surprise you that you cared?

Does it surprise you that you don't care now?

Why are you *really* on this so-called search?

What happened to this Gray person?

What are you *really* going to do on this island?

Why did she want to get rid of you?

Why do you do nothing but think of her?

What do you think she's doing right now?

My dearest wife,
    It is beautiful here, all the water you could want—

He left his hotel room, closed the door on the airless carton, the cube of wood. The hotel was a line of knots in a block of board. He rocked on his heels. Weather vane, water, birds turning in air. Bluefields. It wasn't impossible that she would come. She'd done less likely things. And she was due, he knew, vacation days.

He went down to the dock. He walked on sidewalks raised three feet off the ground, passed houses on stilts, canoes tied up like horses, as if he had arrived at the blue and green land of Noah and everybody knew just who wasn't getting on that ark and it was them and they were ready. He stepped onto the dock, good hand in his pocket. Looked out to the ocean. How far is it anyway, this Corn Island?

Far.

A local woman sat on a little motorboat, a book of pictures in her lap.

How far?

Very. Too far to see. Too far to walk or swim.

How can I get there? Can I take a boat?

There's no boat. A boat would take all day.

Would you take me in your boat?

Who knows when a boat will want to go that way. Not me and my boat.

How, then?

She didn't answer. She bent back over her book, would only look at her pictures and ignore him, but then she sat up and said, Why not fly?

Is there even an airport here?

Yes, of course. Planes all over.

Except I have no money. Almost no money.

Thirty dollars American. Do you have that?

Thirty dollars only?

Myers couldn't believe it. Myers had ninety-two dollars.

Do I need a passport? I have no passport.

Old Joe takes you over. He won't ask much.

Well, why didn't I fly in the first place?

How should I know? No one can know an ignorant mind.

My dearest wife,

On vacation, the scenes turn like pictures on pages—

At the airport in Bluefields, the planes came down like hail and flew up like pollen, spinning overhead, and everyone waited in line for them like for the bus. Myers waited in the small white room with all the other people who wanted to get one of those lifts.

Who's going to Corn Island?

Only Myers raised his hand. Oh, and a few others. A man and a woman with suitcases and hats, a small child with a toy can on a string like a pet.

Fog river. Drizzle. An airstrip of cork and anchor. He boarded a plane made of tinfoil and paint, the size and dull shine of a kitchen appliance. He ducked into the low narrow shell. He fastened himself in and held on.

A vacation is simply, you know, to vacate. The vacationer leaves the home (leaves the mind), leaves the home empty (except for what he left behind (her)), that's all.

No, no, that's not a vacation, if you simply move to a different spot. That's just looking at stuff, familiar stuff.

What's so familiar about this? Myers would certainly like to know.

CLAIRE

I was walking around my apartment. I was back from my trip. I was opening kitchen cabinets and closing them. Food. That would be one element of my new life plan. I would eat like a regular person from now on. Also, location. I would move. What was I still doing here? I'd been sitting around this place all these years, thinking a ghost was going to show up and take care of me—maybe they'd all forgotten I was here. But I could see now that nobody I knew was coming back for their stuff.

Things were going to be different now. I had new circuits in my head. Old switches were directing me to new lines. I'd get a job, I was thinking. Or an activity resembling one. I wouldn't wait here all day until a decent hour to turn up at the bar.

Anything else while I'm at it?

Yep, I was going to go for a walk.

I picked up my bag and left the apartment.

I got on the F train. I wanted ocean spray and boardwalk. I was ready to face the sea air head on. The man who raised me used to take me there as a kid. We ate some pretty tasty things, trodding on those planks—cloud candy, stuffed nuts. I rode to the end of the line and got off at Coney Island.

Myers looked out at the plane's shadow on the water. It was the tiniest plane he'd ever seen and meanwhile the water was an immensity, as if the land had gone, as if this little plane were the only piece left, the last shred of earth, this plaything, torn off and thrown out over the water while the rest of human feats sank below—or had never existed, as if this were the sole output of thousands of years of effort, this little craft, buzzing along without grace or beauty or reason or intent.

Anyway, this is no vacation.

It's vacation enough. Colonial town. Beach. An afternoon in the hotel, writing postcards.

Myers has written no postcards.

Emails then.

The emails have been no vacation.

You get the idea.

The plane chugged on with its propeller of paper clip and glue. An awkward dart, flimsy and small. It seemed barely there between the sky and the sea. Hard to believe he would find earth at the other end, harder that he would find dancing and drinks and song. The plane flew so low that mist or cloud entered the cabin. Myers could see nothing, not his hand in front of his face. Even his thoughts numbed and faded.

The plane landed. Myers stepped down into an empty field. Nothing. Patches of dry grass, some scrappy bushes alongside the airstrip, a bit of tangled barbed wire. A three-wall hut served as the airport. The other people on the plane hadn't gotten off, were getting off someplace else, or maybe they hadn't gotten on at all.

He stood on the airstrip, picked up his briefcase. Walked out to the mud road. Fields all around, not a cat or a church in sight.

Is this Corn Island? he called, wavering, considering the serious lack of billboards, the serious lack of a serious road, as in pavement, as in cement, the serious lack of stores and people and wares. Hello? he called to the pilot, the only man in sight, who was leaning against the plane, reading from the middle of a thick book, his face under the lip of the plane. Which way is town? Myers called. The pilot raised his hand from the book and pointed down the road.

The road was rutted. Great pits had been torn out of it and thrown to the side. He stepped through the mud. Myers, the only tourist in the country who hadn't known there would be no using leather briefcases, winter coats, suitcases with little wheels, forget it. And no wearing shoes like the kind Myers had on, the kind that belonged to a man in an office, the kind that ruined in mud, that stuck there and had to be sucked out, one by one. He tramped on.

Somehow a taxi had been dispatched and was bumping around the corner. It took a while to get to Myers because it had to sort of climb over the hills of clay and rise up out of the ditches. Myers waited for it to travel the hundred or so yards to him, until it finally arrived and stopped.

Downtown, please, said Myers.

Downtown? Where is that?

The business district.

Business?

Like for buying.

Buying what?

Take me to the tourist section. The place with the hotels and restaurants, the Internet cafés.

Oh, Internet. There is no Internet here.

No Internet?

No Internet? Then how could Gray have emailed...

This may have been the last moment Myers would entertain the notion of finding Gray, although truthfully his hope had already faded. There were plenty of people looking for Gray. They were trolling the earth with their questions and notepads.

And regarding the wife coming?

He got it already, all right? Don't be sassy.

CLAIRE

I stepped out to the boardwalk. Was this Coney Island? Not the happy spot I recalled. It seemed small and huddled now. The planks were cracked. The shop awnings torn. Trash was piled up in places as if the trash men came only when paid. It didn't matter. I felt tall and new. I felt mended among broken objects. I stayed on my feet and watched my step.

I stopped in at the freak show. It was in a very bad way. The tightrope walker fell. The impresario was gone, run away. The fire eater was a hysterical drunk and the magician was giving away her tricks for a buck. I left. A lingering dog followed me out. I kept going.

Across the boardwalk, the sea was a dull tin plate. Shards of glass and rocks washed up onshore. A stubborn decay had lodged in the sand.

I came to a white wall, an entry gate, a building of postwar cement. It was pushed back from the boardwalk. A kid out front was trying to sell me his bottle of water. What is that? I said, nodding at the building.

The aquarium.

Oh. I had forgotten it was there. I went over to the kiosk.

Tickets half-price, said the lady. Half-price or less. Make me an offer. Seahorses. Spiderfish. Get your last glimpse.

Why last?

Condemned. They're tearing down the whole town next month. Taking away the Ferris wheel in crates.

I checked my pockets. I've got two dollars, I said.

Isn't that the dog from the freak show? she said.

I shrugged.

She stamped my ticket. The dog stays outside, she said.

Consider. At this point Myers could wind up in many possible positions (as one winds a watch or a top and then lets go). Many futures were still possible, if he managed to live beyond the falling-curtain end of his vacation, if he turned up alive, didn't throw himself off a coast guard ship sixty knots out into the sea in the middle of a hurricane.

One possible future was that his wife could come to Corn Island and they'd have the loveliest vacation yet and then go back to New York on the same plane. This option hung on a wall hook in Myers's mind, though he knew it was not hanging anyplace else (her mind, for example). If he continued to live, he'd move through his days, wondering if they'd reunite, creating scenarios in his mind, in the same way some people wonder if certain buildings will collapse or keep standing, or if the person sleeping beside them is the person they married and not some cheap replacement brought in and forced to pretend. Each morning Myers would rise and ask the following: Had he glimpsed her in the past [week, month, year] (check one)? Or if not her, someone who knew her? Looked like her? Had he spoken to anyone in the past [week, month, year] who had ever spoken to her? Did she have any direct impact today on anything having to do with him or affecting him, say, political events or new discoveries? What did she have to do with the weather today? Were there any other miscellaneous mysteries that joined them—had they both opened their takeout Chinese cookies at the same moment last night perhaps and found the same lucky number printed on the paper inside?

So the possibility would exist in his mind and questions such as these would fill his nights.

The roads were oceanic. The taxi rode up the crests and slid down the other side. They went to place after place. They drove through pockets of trees, came out onto water and falling sun. Here and there, a house on stilts. They didn't see any downtown but they didn't stop trying.

Here is the downtown, said the cabman.

This isn't downtown, said Myers and he knew he had to be right. A worn façade of battered wood. No one in sight. COCA-COLA read a sign, bleached and shot.

Keep going, said Myers. We're almost there. The next one is it.

If you say so, said the cabman.

Second option. He could meet someone else, marry again. Someone he could fight with more fully and be left by more fully. This time she might leave in a direct fashion—no puttering around with hesitations, vacations, the mewling of emails and phone calls. She'd be gone by dawn, reinstalled elsewhere, a note left behind on his desk. So instead of stretching out of this shape of despair, Myers could curl further in.

CLAIRE

I wandered in. I walked through a twist of rooms filled with water and bright staring creatures trapped in cubes of light. The place was empty of people. The fork fish were sunk in the coral. A turtle was paddling against the glass, churning, making a slow getaway. The octopus had skin like folded cloth.

I stepped around a corner and came upon a pair of animals ricocheting off the walls of their seabox. A piece of food came down as if dropped from the sky and one of them swooped in and snapped it. Dolphins.

Of course. I couldn't just let it go. Not me. I had to go straight to the only ones in New York, as far as I knew. Tendencies like this have a name. I'm a plant turning toward light. A leaf of me will always reach for my father. It was okay. I stepped right up to the glass. The dolphins slid by my face. In fact, they were kind of appealing. Hi guys, I said. What are you doing in there?

Third option. His wife could wind up with another man.

Which man? Gray, or someone else?

Whoever. There are plenty of men.

Finally he got out. Had to. They'd been twice across the island and still had found nothing Myers wanted and the cabman had to go home. We came close, said Myers. They had. A small string of stores selling plastic battleships, encyclopedias, limes.

Not close enough for you to get out, said the cabman, which was true.

(What had Myers wanted?)

Fourth option. He could wind up alone. Its own great tragedy, that.

He paid and got out. He had forty-eight dollars and a collection of córdobas and coins that he wasn't sure what to do with exactly, how to offer them, how many of them to hold out or withhold.

He was at the far end of the island, a few huts set up by the water. Loud sea, landslide of sand. He leaned in the window. Don't leave me here, he said.

Why not? said the cabman. He gestured. It's beautiful.

I don't know that word, said Myers.

The taxi thumped off.

The part about the money: He managed to rent a cabin for eleven dollars a night, which meant he had four nights and four dollars leftover before ruin set in for good—four nights if he didn't want to eat anything or go anywhere or spend more than a dollar a day, which he might not have to do because the island had no Internet and no phone and nothing else to do. And the owner made him a little soup because there were no restaurants within walking distance and anyway there were no lights on the road and you couldn't walk in that unless you wanted to fall into a hole, and no taxis came out this far without prior arrangement, which had to be done by some secret means—word of mouth, sky signals, fax—a day in advance since there was no phone and anyway no restaurant would be open this time of night or open at all without prior arrangement and the owner explained all this and then made him some soup or gave him the soup that she had and he started to eat it but then he did not because unfamiliar, once-living things floated in it and came up with the spoon. So he just sat by the water.

What are you doing here? the owner wanted to know. She came out to ask him, wiping her hands on her skirt.

The sky looked like a kite blowing away.

Myers would rather not say.

He could wind up in other ways too. Most he imagined involved him ruined, him waiting, trying to get somewhere and never arriving, trying to convince someone, failing. But there were other possibilities too. Some leaky but seaworthy. There were some good ones, more hopeful, blinking on in the distance. They floated around like tin ships.

It was that night that for the final time Myers saw himself finding Gray. Although his conscious mind had given up, his dream mind held out a slim hope. Gray came to him in his sleep. He showed up in the cabin doorway, leaned in, and flicked on the light—which would not have been possible, of course, since the lights worked on a generator and switched off at ten.

I knew it had to be you, Gray said. What other gringo would show up on this island and dance the Bus Stop all night?

He wore an old-style grin.

The owner was doing her part, she really was, and he knew it because after the soup, she came out again. She held up a cassette player and a tape. Dancing? she said. Anyone for dancing?

Myers waved her off.

Oh, he doesn't know how to dance, *pobrecito*. What with all those bandages.

Doesn't know how to dance, excuse me? Hadn't he danced at his own wedding for four hours straight? He had, thank you very much. The wedding had been a real one, if anyone wondered. They'd had ice sculptures and centerpieces, a photographer, a videographer, an extra hour of open bar. They'd had seventy witnesses, most still alive today. People who had seen him dance and applauded.

Myers stood, bowed.

So she put in that tape and they danced in the sand. She had only one tape and it had only one song but it happened to be the Bus Stop, which Myers knew and even with his bad arm could do. They rewound and rewound and she ran and got her kids and her husband and they ran and got their cousins and uncles and friends, and other people came wandering over, came into the circle of light, raised their hands. And they all danced the Bus Stop.

In the dream, Gray said the bit about the Bus Stop, then he grinned, then he did a little stepping around himself, right around the room, Myers, laughing, up on an elbow, in bed. And there were no trinkets, no sights, no birding, no language class. Nobody got onto water skis. But guess what.

The true fun began.

Walk up and down. Dip.

Step to the side, step back. Clap.

Chapter Nineteen

The true fun did not begin, however. In the morning Myers woke, examined his smarting arm, his bruised ribs, left his room.

The true fun did not begin because Gray was in Panama nearly dead by that time and soon completely dead, and the closest Myers would come to him was years later, long after Myers was completely dead himself. It wasn't Gray who came close in any case but Gray's small daughter. Years later she set out on her search.

The true fun did not begin that morning or ever. Not for Myers. He walked off down the beach.

So.

The only boat that seemed to be leaving the island and not going back to the mainland was a coast guard boat that no one could see because it wasn't there. It was on its way, coming through the waters, heading toward the island. Myers heard about it and thought he should look for it, or actually look for its future spot of departure, and for its leaders, those in charge when it would strike for open sea, because he wasn't going to turn around and go back the way he'd come. And he wasn't going to just stand there and dry up like a crab—he'd come this far already. He'd go all the way.

He heard about the boat because someone was walking around making promises about it, and while he didn't see anybody making the promises, he did hear the promises themselves. The owner of his residence told him and she said the promises were deep and long, like the wake a ship cuts as it steers away from shore.

How do I find this man?

The owner didn't say, and it was another piece of information Myers wasn't going to get, but then she said, Look, here he comes now, and there the man was, walking in the sand.

It turned out Myers had seen him already, early in the morning, but he had thought he was dreaming, thought he was still sleeping and thinking of Gray approaching for his last step-around. The man had been coming over the sand in white clothing. He had come from far away and he was walking in a ray of light shooting through an edge of the clouds. A string of dogs followed behind.

The man took a seat at a table made of straw. Myers went over to him. May I talk to you?

Okay, you got me, he said. He raised his hands as if in surrender. You want an autograph? A picture?

Myers thought about it.

What are you famous for?

Fourteen years later, Gray's small daughter, still small but less small, bought a plane ticket and went to Nicaragua to look for her father, though she had barely known him and had not seen him since she was four. She wouldn't have recognized him if she came on him unless he looked exactly as he did in the two photos she had of him, that is, if he wore a striped, collared shirt and was turned to the right, or if he had on roller skates and was holding her, miniature-sized and also on skates, by the hand.

I steal dolphins, said the man.

Good idea, said Myers.

I put them back in the sea.

That way they won't run away, Myers said. Hey, I'm here about a boat.

What do you want a boat for? the untrainer said. Land's fine. Beach, sand.

I'd like a little more than sand.

You want more, stick around, my friend.

I'd prefer not to stay.

I'm just saying. Things are going to heat up a bit around here.

It's already plenty hot.

All I'm saying, he said, there's going to be additional action around here tomorrow.

What are you talking about, tomorrow? said Myers. This place is a salty grave.

Tomorrow. The untrainer thrust his chin toward the huts. This place'll be packed. No room for anyone. They'll be doubling up. Better reserve your room.

A cruise ship is coming?

A cruise ship, ha! Run for your life. No, no goddamn cruise ship comes through here.

Then what?

Government.

Is that all? said Myers. They're already here. They're somewhere, they're everywhere.

Even without the Internet, Myers could still hear his wife, could still call to her, and could still receive her declarations, though they came blown in, downwind, delayed, bony, full of dust: *My dearest husband, On holiday some hear better than others, some see better than others, some move by touch alone. Sometimes in large churches, people are crushed beneath them and can't pull themselves out. Sometimes people tumble into the sea and are drowned. Whether they choose to call this vacation or salvation depends on their own hearts and conscience.*

Your wife yet

Gray's small daughter went from place to place in a country she had no idea her father had never seen. As it happens, she went to the same places Myers had visited. She favored the tourist spots first because it seemed reasonable: what else could her father have intended other than the trip as vacation, the chance for some sun and some sea? She walked through Managua, rode on day trips out of town, and later visited the tourist islands, the larger ones of the lake and one of the ones in the Atlantic. She didn't carry the two photos for comparison and she didn't ask anyone if they'd seen him because it had been so long by that time, no one could have remembered him. She walked around with her pack on, her sandals on, her bottle of water in a bag, her mosquito hat, her mosquito net. She had all the proper equipment that Myers had lacked. She stopped at regular intervals and thought about her father, tried to know him by looking at things she believed he might have seen. She stood in spots Myers himself had stood, Myers also thinking of Gray and also of another person whom he too had once known and had lost.

So it wasn't quite what anybody expected or wanted but still in a way Myers was followed by Gray (or at least his daughter) (albeit years later), and still in a way Gray's daughter followed her dad (or someone who knew him, sort of).

Well, anyway.

Look, I'm wondering if you'll take me with you on the boat that's coming. I hear you're the man in charge.

You know where that boat is going?

It doesn't matter.

Nowhere. Not to any destination you could plant your feet in. That boat is going out into the sea.

That's okay.

It'll be crowded too.

I have no luggage. Okay, I have a little luggage.

No luggage.

I'll leave it.

SPOKE

Yes, I did go to that island. I arrived one day and left the next. And I only stayed that long because there was just one plane a day.

When I got there, I stepped off the plane onto an apocalyptic landscape. I don't know why that should have surprised me. Not one thing has been like anyone described it and that is partly understandable, but you would have thought they'd get at least a little close on some counts. There was nothing in sight. I thought I'd been dropped off on the moon. Dry grasses, spreading landscape, the most vacant scene of a lifetime. I wish I could say it was a relief after the mainland but it was awful. I felt like they'd dumped me, the whole country. Didn't want me there so they made me leave, talked me into it. One might almost suspect they were playing a trick on me or a game involving many people and pieces and places and an enormous amount of coordination and even specially printed papers, fake machines with lights on them, coded bills passed by my own hands into those of a player that would direct him to the next move. And I was foolish. I'd believed every word they said. I've been listening to people for so long my ears hurt. Anyone can see that Corn Island is a practically deserted island, not a romping tourist spot. I was so tired of having to explain the sounds and pictures in my head. All I did was look astonished at the sky, look astonished at the ground. I picked up my suitcase. I was the only passenger on the airplane—that should have been a hint. I walked through the grass toward what seemed to be a mud road. I arrived at the road and kept walking.

I suppose I can always keep a spare gringo around. Now and then I need a hand.

I've got that. Myers lifted his good one.

So the untrainer and Myers walked off over the hot sand, over kilometers of it, under the sun that split the clouds, to the secret hiding place, which turned out to be the sea, and who knows why they had to come out this far, all the way to the edge of really nothing from what wasn't much to start, who knows, and Myers said so.

You could have brought the whole operation a little closer, he said.

It's for safety. From theft.

Theft of what?

The dolphin.

My God, what paranoia, said Myers. What does anyone want with a dolphin? Then he said, Oh look.

And he said this because he could suddenly see it, there in the water. Its fin skirted the surface, then dove below.

My dearest wife...

My dearest husband,

Some vacations end when we least expect it. Some vacations are a matter of taking matters into one's hands and stopping it right there. Some operate like the moon, waxing and waning. Vacations come in all sorts: the overdue, the one-stop,

the unlikely. You decide when it's done.
   Your loving wife

Gray's small daughter never came close to Panama, never learned about
her father's demise and about the woman who closed his eyelids, which
she herself should have closed with her own hand. She had, for the rest
of her life, a longing for the man she recalled only as having played
airplane with her every other weekend, lifting her up off the floor, until
he disappeared. She'd smiled fiercely as he zoomed her around. She had
felt the power of flight.

Back in his hut Myers wrote another email in his head, sent it through
the crack in his skull. Notes of apology, of absolution. He wrote another,
and another, wrote emails in felt-tip, in highlighter, wrote to everyone
he could think of whom he'd disappointed, not shown up for, failed, or
who had failed him.

CLAIRE
   I watched the dolphins in the tank. They scooted around. I tried
to feel something. I knew I was supposed to feel something—jealousy,
maybe, that my father had chosen them over me. But I didn't. I was
lighthearted. They spun in the water like flexible metal sheeting.
   A spiral staircase was cemented to the side of the tank. I walked up
it, holding onto the handrail, a motor purr under my feet. I stepped up
into a huge room with the waxy appearance of the moon. Across the
surface of the pool sat a set of white bleachers and between them was a
small man in a green jumpsuit. He was the first person I'd seen inside
the aquarium. He had a bucket in his hand. He took a fish from it and
hurled it into the water.
   He saw me and looked disgusted. Who let you in here? he said.

Myers still had a few more items he had to decide what to do about, and those included the contents of his briefcase, which he dinged into the wastebasket, and then the briefcase itself, not too hard, he just opened the door and threw it out into the sand. Some other fool might come in having dropped out of the sky with things to hang onto and nowhere to put them and this case might be of use.

There.

The song of Myers's heart thudded on the fretboard.

He went out and got the empty briefcase and brought it back inside.

He opened the door and threw it out.

Chapter Twenty

The part about the people coming: In the morning an airplane brought four taxis-full bumping up the road. Then a second plane flew in overhead and the owner said she couldn't believe it. What is more amazing than more than one plane a day. Myers saw that indeed there was going to be no empty beach today. More taxis and more taxis came, bringing sea divers and vets from Costa Rica, newspaper reporters with computers and microphones, and one poor local with a notepad and a pen. Then a helicopter landed, blowing the palm trees and plastic chairs, and a film crew and photographers from *Discover This!* sprang out. They began setting up their boxy equipment and shooting photos of everything in sight—the dogs, the plants, the sand. Some of them flapped around in wet suits, holding underwater cameras.

Where's the dolphin? they wanted to know. What are we here for if not the dolphin?

Another helicopter landed, and then another, one carrying the Nicaraguan minister of the environment and the other the minister of the sea, stylish men in loose suits, along with their bodyguards and advisors. Then another landed and several women in bikinis stepped out. They stood neatly on either side of the ministers and fed them bits of fish for the cameras. Then the skinny dolphin trainer who had originally plucked the dolphin out of the sea appeared and was arguing for his rights. Finally the Nicaraguan coast guard pulled up in a ship and rode a fleet of tiny boats to shore and suddenly the place was crowded with military.

How were they going fit all these people on the boat and Myers too? He didn't know.

Overhead it was a solar eclipse or the end of the world or maybe just a clouded-over sky.

Besides the obvious—the coats, the suitcase, the minor luggage—there were other things to track as well, if anyone wanted to follow him, which no one did, apparently. Things mostly made of paper—the dollars and córdobas spent, the bills picked up and put down on tables, torn bus tickets, receipts, brochures that described the way to one place, the way away from another, a couple of English-language newspapers. And the trail was made up of other materials too. Footprints in mud, his password entered into computers, his passport number in registers, plus pieces of the body—hair strands, nail parings, saliva on pillows.

A shout went up. Where is the dolphin? We want to see the dolphin.

All right, I'll show you, said the untrainer. But you have to promise not to get in the water.

What are you talking about? said the men in wet suits with cameras, said the women in bikinis, said the vet and the coast guard. All had brought their swim trunks. Swim with the dolphin. Set the dolphin free.

Forget it. No one's seeing him.

All right, they said. We promise not to get in the water. Really, we won't. We swear. May we see the dolphin now?

Not, he said, unless I have everyone's word on their life.

On our lives, they said. They each had to say it, one by one.

Then they began the long trek over the sand. They started out proudly like a procession, some of them marching at the front, the ones at the back singing a song. Myers walked in the middle.

Where are your hats? the untrainer said. Put on your hats. Bring water.

It's not even sunny, they said. It's going to rain. We'll be fine. We're fine. Just bring us to the fish.

They went on.

CLAIRE

Well? said the man with the bucket. Who let you in?

The woman in the ticket booth, I said.

Show's over. Shoo.

These are business hours, I said. You're open.

He made a sound in his throat. He was looking at me, carefully. He was about the same age as me. My mind ticked: Nope, not my father.

Are these yours? I said. I walked forward, pointed to the tank. Are you the ringmaster?

He overhanded a fish into the water, watched me.

I leaned over a plastic plaque. I see one of them won an award, I said. Which one is Sunbeam?

Stupid name, he said. Not my idea.

A dolphin came up for air and upset the water between us.

So someone else named them? I said.

These bad boys are mine, he said. I taught them how to do somersaults.

I've seen some do cartwheels.

They can do a jig in the air on their tails.

Pretty neat trick. If all you've got is a tail.

They came here wild as sperm, he said. I've been with them since day one. They know my voice. I know theirs.

This place is shutting down, I said. I walked a little closer. What's going to happen to them?

Stop right there, he said.

I stopped.

What are you doing here? he said.

They began to slow down. Nobody was fine. How far is it? they said. They were squinting and sweating. The filmmakers were putting down their bags, sitting. How much longer, do you think?

You goddamn people, the untrainer said. He threw his hat in the sand. The stupidest people I ever saw in my life.

Oh, we're very sorry. They got to their feet.

The untrainer picked up his hat. He passed around his bottle of water and so did Myers. They all resumed the walk, crowdedly, quieter, until they arrived.

Other articles to track: what's not there—the indentations in beds, on seats, empty spaces where Myers once had been, spaces not yet filled by another, the space in a particular corner of the bus station where he had stood for one hour and twenty minutes, the space under a tree where he had sought shade for a few moments while he looked up a fact in his guidebook. Myers is gone but the air still bends around his shape as air does around all shapes that once lived in it. Also spaces on shelves from where he removed objects, such as the pack of batteries he bought for his razor, the sunblock, the food off the plates, the hole in the hen's heart for the egg he ate for breakfast.

So how do you feel? a reporter asked the vet.

Well, I'll tell you, said the vet. There's always tension about moving an animal, but we have a plan for everything and an alternate plan for everything else.

A few poles stuck out of the water. It was taking a while to see even a little bit of dolphin. It hardly surfaced anymore, just to catch a breath.

The coast guard was handing out life jackets and people were putting them on. Myers couldn't fit his over the sling. He carried it around and then set it down and lost track of it. One of the sea divers had his equipment on upside down. Nobody wanted to tell him.

Film me, said the sea diver. Why aren't you filming me?

This is about protocol, said the vet. That is the essential part. You have to meet with the navy, the army, the government. You have to look at the supplies, the nets. But the main thing is the protocol, how to move the animal, how to hold the animal.

The film equipment was sinking in the sand.

CLAIRE

What do you want? said the man. You have business here?

For a moment I couldn't speak.

My father died, I peeped.

So what. Fathers die.

He wasn't my real father.

Nobody raises their own kids anymore.

I know who my real father is.

Everyone has a father.

No, it's him, I said. I opened my bag and found the photo. I stepped forward, held it out. What do you think of that? This man is my father. How about that? The one with the hoop.

He set down his bucket, removed a pair of glasses from his jumpsuit pocket. Put them on and looked at the photo. He took them off and looked at me.

You're meeting him here? he said.

It seemed to Myers that everyone had to be there by then, what with all those people milling around, but everyone wasn't. Some people were still on the coast guard boat because they sailed by, waving and pointing at themselves so they would get filmed too, and someone was in a truck because it came riding over the sand and stopped. Then another boat showed up full of mattresses and the soldiers dragged the mattresses out of the boat and dropped them, first in the water, then in the sand. They put the mattresses in the back of the truck. Then they took out a yellow stretcher and entered the water. They slid the stretcher under the net. They moved forward bit by bit, closing the net—the dolphin swimming back and forth, and the untrainer too, swimming back and forth—until the net was a small bubble and the dolphin was thrashing and not getting in the stretcher like he was supposed to.

What are we going to do? the soldiers said. We'll never get him in the stretcher.

The untrainer said, Would you idiots get out of my way? And he took the dolphin and put him in the stretcher.

Nobody had ever seen anything like that in their life, they all agreed, the way he put that animal there.

Meanwhile, it started to rain.

On Myers, if anyone is interested: If he were to survive this and not die in deep water, he would eventually find his way back to New York, would eventually let curiosity burn in through the crack in his skull and he would wander back to her apartment, the suspended box that they had once shared. He would stand outside in the cold and look up and see a light in the window. Instead of strolling away or ringing the bell, he would sneak around the back, climb the fire escape. He'd have to jump to grab the ladder, would twice fall in the snow. But the third time he'd make it, would pull the ladder down and hoist himself up. He'd walk up to their floor and peer in the window. He'd be ready to run or ready to break in the window shouting, the choice depending on his own unknowable reactions, not on whatever he saw there—he would assume he would see her with Gray (an absurd idea, since she hadn't seen Gray in years and anyway he was dead, but Myers, also dead by this time, would never know that). None of this will happen, but if it did, she would be there alone, curled on the couch, a single lamp lit, the TV flashing blue on her face.

If he had seen that, it would have proved nothing to him, of course. She could have been living with Gray or another man who could be out for the evening, at his own supposed meeting, following someone else, coming home any minute. He could have already gone to bed and she, sleepless, had stayed up a half hour longer. It could mean the man had rejected her and now she was lying there, lonely and sad, missing him, not Myers. Myers would watch as long as he dared, fog the window, twice raise his hand to knock, twice lower it. He would crawl back down, drop into the snow.

If he had made it back, he would have done it once more —not to his wife, not her (his) apartment, but someone else's, another woman, two years after that, and this time she, the other she, the new she, *would* be with someone else, a man, also normal-looking like Gray, but not Gray, and the two of them would be sitting side by side, also on a couch, also watching TV, and the moment would look so drab and unintimate that it would be almost impossible to be jealous but Myers would manage.

Despite these behaviors appropriate only to grief, even Myers would not have spent his life alone.

But none of this happens. Myers never winds up alive on dry land again.

So the untrainer slid the dolphin into the yellow stretcher and then the soldiers carried the stretcher to the truck bed and put it on top of the wet mattresses. Then they slung their machine guns onto their backs and got in. Myers got in too because the untrainer waved at him and yelled for him to through the rain. Because it was now raining hard.

And then they were off.

Or not quite, because the truck wouldn't start. It stalled—the driver trying to turn over the engine, the dolphin whistling, everyone screaming through the rain. Then it started and people cheered and they were off. Or not quite, because then the truck got stuck in the sand, which was turning into mud. The police and the soldiers and the bystanders and even the vets and the sea divers from Costa Rica and even the minister of the environment and the minister of the sea, even the wicked dolphin trainer himself pushed the truck, and it moved at last. They cheered.

CLAIRE

What do you mean? You know where he is?

He won't be here for a few hours, the man said. You can wait. There's a chair over there.

I should go, I said, alarmed. I walked back toward the stairs. I have to go, I said.

Suit yourself. I don't care.

Okay, goodbye, I said. But I stopped. Under the windowpane of water, a dolphin went by like a submarine.

I turned back. What's he coming for?

He gave a laugh. They think they're going to send my two buddies to a water park? Not my Sunbeam. Who knows what kind of jerk'll be in charge at a place like that. No, I need to bring in a specialist. Someone I can trust.

You'll get in big trouble for this.

He picked up the bucket. You don't surrender what's yours, he said. He lifted a fish over the pool.

I didn't move. Would you introduce me? I said.

A daughter doesn't need an introduction.

We've never met.

That's no way to treat your old man. A handsome dolphin leapt and crisply removed the fish from his hand, slid back into the water.

Sit, he said. I'll introduce you.

You believe me? I said. That he's my father. Why?

Lady, you look exactly like him.

Oh, I said. I looked at the photo in my hand. It was true. The fact of it came skidding around the bend. I put down my bag. I sat down to wait.

At the last moment she must have heard him. Somehow his call entered her mind because early that morning Myers's wife woke having dreamed of water. She walked through the apartment. It had a soaked look, drenched, as if it had been long dunked. Her own things looked unfamiliar, wetter. A submerged thought rose to the top. There is something wrong with me, she thought. Something that is not wrong with most people.

It turned out that Myers knew his wife better than most would give him credit for, because that morning she sat down at her computer and booked a three-pronged flight to Corn Island (Houston, Managua, Corn), leaving a few minutes later for the airport. Why? Because in the moisture the stone of her heart had eroded into sand, which is softer. She saw herself without him, saw her nights in front of the TV. She knew this was her chance to go after something at last. And if it wasn't the perfect thing for her, for either of them, at least it was an attempt. She charged $2,399 to her credit card, packed a change of clothing in her purse even though she could already see what would happen. With the first snowflakes of winter in the sky, she headed out in a taxi.

The dolphin whistled in the busted truck. The rain came down. The photographers and the reporters ran behind the truck in their life jackets, waving pieces of foam. A line of taxis came behind. The truck drove to the end of the dock. The soldiers and the untrainer hoisted the dolphin off the truck, onto the boat, and into a large foam container.

The photographers got on the boat.

The reporters got on the boat.

The vets and sea divers from Costa Rica got on the boat.

The soldiers from the coast guard got on the boat.

The minister of the environment and the minister of the sea got on the boat.

The sexy women in bikinis got on the boat.

Some people who looked like waiters got on the boat.

Myers got on the boat.

The skinny dolphin trainer was not allowed on the boat. He stayed on the dock, his hands opening and closing.

In the category of regrets: Mostly vague and imprecise, having to do with his childhood (window, head, ground) and adulthood (wife, man, briefcase), mostly a cloud moving over the waters, darkening it section by section. There were also the regrets about his abilities, about his activities, the regrets about his injured mind. Also sentences he had said and ones he hadn't, blocks he had walked in certain directions, a man he wished he'd been, a woman he wished he'd understood, demands not made, promises kept, a raincoat he'd pulled from taxi doors.

You couldn't say he was going out after the dolphin, that he was the sort of man who couldn't keep his seat, had to go flinging himself out after any animal that happened to be leaving, since that would require that the dolphin went first and it didn't. He was very particular about that.

There were a lot of people on the boat, plus the dolphin, and the boat was not that big. People were screaming because the rain was really coming down now. It was thundering. It was a storm, maybe a very big storm. People were screaming because they couldn't be heard, because they were getting wet, very wet, because they were scared to go out on the ocean in a storm like this. What were they, crazy? Look at it out there. It looked like hurricane. Was it a hurricane? Look at those waves.

Maybe we should do this tomorrow, someone yelled through the storm.

Tomorrow, tomorrow, everyone said.

What? Are you insane? the untrainer said. The wind whipped his hair. I won't be here tomorrow. Don't you dare move. You stay where you are, he said. Everybody, stay where you are. Let's go.

Tomorrow, of course, the untrainer would be on a plane to New York.

It's silly to think Gray died of a broken heart when he died of a broken brain. Gray had plenty of broken parts on him by that time, but he also had parts that would have kept working, given the chance. He had parts that would have worked for a thousand years and others that would have worked for a hundred, and others for another year or two or perhaps a bit more. Some of him may still be working somewhere in one way or another. If you count the girl—she *is* his, after all—she is still working, fifty weeks a year at a small thermagraphic printing shop in an upscale neighborhood in Philadelphia. Wave bye-bye.

Bye-bye.

Myers's wife didn't make it to Corn Island in time to see her husband. She caught her connection in Houston, landed in Managua. She walked through the airports swiftly on strong legs. She boarded the flight to Corn and then sat on the runway for three hours past the time of scheduled departure. Storm, they said. Hurricane on the coast. They waited three hours, served two rounds of drinks and some snacks in small foiled bags. She did not help herself to any snacks but she did sip tepid water from a plastic cup and tap her fingernails against the tray table. She only spoke once—when the delay was first announced over the loudspeaker. Damn it to hell, she said, and put her forehead on her fist. They waited until the hurricane moved off and then they went to Corn Island.

At first it wasn't so bad despite the rain and the waves, but the farther they went the worse it got. The large foam container with the dolphin in it began to slip on the deck and hit the chains, which were the only obstacles keeping it from going overboard. People fell over as the boat tipped from side to side and dunked into holes and slammed into waves. The bodyguards tied the women and the ministers to the boat with thick heavy ropes. The waves splashed in and sprayed. The film crew was gone, hidden in the engine room, and the waiters, who had been hired apparently to hand out hors d'oeuvres, were screaming through the storm, throwing cans of soda at people, throwing pieces of cooked fish and raw oysters in an effort to do their jobs. Everyone wore a life jacket except Myers. The untrainer stayed beside the dolphin, waving people away. He slid along with the container, slid through the circle of spectators and back.

Myers's wife stepped off the plane with the same steady stride she'd had all her life. She did not take a taxi, though it was nearing dark. She did not stop strangers and describe her husband or hold up her hand to estimate his height. She walked the length of the island, picked her way over the devastation of the hurricane, over the giant fronds and trunks and pieces of roofing. She went by way of the beach. She passed a person here and there with a wheelbarrow or a cart piled high with torn leafage. She walked all the way around the island.

It was in front of some huts that she found his briefcase. She nearly tripped over it in the sand, the rectangular prison of her husband's soul. She picked it up and looked inside. His. Empty. She understood what she'd done and she felt a white spot in her mind begin to spread.

There was a large gathering a little further up the beach. She took the briefcase and walked over to them. The people seemed to be celebrating in the wreckage, passing large plates of rice down the table, their faces lit by candles. She paused, turned to them, felt she might ask them about her husband, that they might have an idea. Somehow she knew this and her breath felt caught. She pulled herself together and spoke up.

Um, does anybody here speak English?

They surveyed her. A few of us have what is called an education, yeah, why?

Did any of you happen to see the owner of this briefcase? She held it up like a handshake.

Well, not unless we're looking at her.

All right, she said and lowered the briefcase. She was red-eyed, wind-bent. Standing in the sand, she unwished the last three years, those misspent squares of time. Myers's wife. She would be alone.

She kept walking. She went all night. In the morning she arrived back at the popsicle-stand airport. She stood around until a plane came and then she left, went back to New York. Goodbye, wife.

CLAIRE

I was sitting, waiting in the chair like he'd told me to. I'd been waiting about an hour, I think. He brought me a packet of crackers at one point. Then he came over and said he had something to show me. Today's paper, he said. He had a newspaper in his hand and held it out. The front page of the Lifestyles section. A dolphin released yesterday in the middle of a hurricane. There was a little map and a photo of the hero on the shore and in the photo, I couldn't believe it. First I couldn't believe it and then I couldn't believe it again. There was my father on the front page, and beside him a dog in the sand. He looked just like me. I wasn't afraid or full of longing—Oh, at last I'll find out who I am, and all that. Wow, I was thinking. Look at me. He's going to bust in here and light this place up. And I'll have a ringside seat to the show.

In the photo in the newspaper, there in the background, if you looked closely it seemed as if that man with the strangely shaped head was there. You couldn't tell about his head from the photo but it was him. He looked like the man who raised me. He had some sort of wrapping around his arm now. In the foreground was my father, suited for swimming, standing on sand. The two of them together.

There are many ways to see the world.

The thing about the head is that at first it seems normal. You have to keep looking to be sure. Once you're certain, then the question is: how did it get that way? You have to keep staring to imagine all the possible birth defects, personal genetic encounters, public catastrophes that could have done this. You hope he didn't feel it.

It was hours before anyone noticed he was gone. First there was the heroic ride back to shore through the hurricane. Then the entire shipful of people running from the ship, down the dock, across the sand, in search of shelter—people sprinting, yelling, palm trees uprooting, shingles flying. Then, hours later, after the storm, the gathering for the celebratory dinner, people knocking on his cabin door, sitting down to eat. Then the gringa walking up and going away, drifting into the dark with her little suitcase. Then someone saying, Wait, where is he, the gringo? going back, knocking on his cabin door again, Hello? Hello? Then someone else saying, He didn't by any chance have a briefcase, did he? Then the slow realization that no one had seen him since the godforsaken filmmakers took their brave walk.

Chapter Twenty-One

The boat wasn't there yet but they were going to throw the dolphin in. Word came from the back or the front. It's too dangerous, said the captain. It's a hurricane. Throw the fish in. We're turning around or we'll die.

Turn the boat around. Head back, everyone said, shouting down the untrainer. For God's sake, get us back alive!

The vet and one of the sea divers began to argue about how to throw the dolphin in. They had a sort of pulley idea involving a contraption with ropes.

You people are out of your minds. I never saw such stupidity, such incompetence in all my life, said the untrainer. What have I done, letting you idiots on this ship. I'm surprised you haven't sunk it. I should have hired the tooth fairy. I should have hired Tinkerbell.

Okay, big shot, then what are we supposed to do? They were tangled up in the pulley and both were tied to the boat.

The untrainer directed the soldiers and the bodyguards to pick up the stretcher and carry it over to the side of the boat. The dolphin jumped into the ocean and swam away.

Oh! they said. He's in the water. Is he okay? Will he make it?

And far off, amazingly, they saw him, the dolphin. He jumped high in the air, made giant arcs over the water, two arcs, then two more, and then he was gone. Everyone saw it, everyone cheered—except Myers, who was already gone.

(One small man plinks off the earth, vanishes silently into water.)

His feet had to have a steady moment before liftoff, but "liftoff" is a rather fancy phrasing for how it happened. It was more like stepping overboard. But we do not say he stepped overboard or walked as though there were a plank involved—there certainly was not. Also the irony of the final steadying: Why steady himself? Why bother? But it does make sense if you think about it. You don't want to fall over accidentally, hit your head, and roll back into the boat, or have your foot get caught on the chain and be left swinging and be saved, or be saved but hurt, more than you already are, and have the dolphin go off without you, or have it be a question: did he trip and fall overboard or did he jump of his own accord? If the thing would happen, it required this moment of steadying, this last decision. I will do this, I will go.

And about the chain, there was that to be gotten over, no small trick, a swinging chain, a tossing boat, a broken arm, broken ribs, a hurricane on the horizon. He had to grasp the chain with his good hand and get one leg over it and then the other. The chain—whoever thought a thing like that could keep anyone in? A flimsy piece of metal, what was it even doing there?

(Time to go.)

(Myers first.)

When a dolphin slides into water, it is different, of course. A single movement, a semicircle, a flash of muscle, and then it's done.

Question: did anyone see him go over?

SEXY WOMAN IN BIKINI

I had a rope around my waist and I knew very well that the plan had not included any storm or rope, and I had no sense of humor about it. I don't believe anyone did. I did not see one person laugh and I saw plenty of faces, I assure you. I did see the gringo come around the side with the photographers behind him. I don't know who that gringo was or how he'd gotten on the boat. But I do remember him because there was something wrong with his head and his arm was in a sling. He was a mess. I remember thinking he should have a life jacket on and should be tied down like the rest of us and not leading the photographers around, who should have been tied down too. I didn't look at him much. I was watching the photographers with their cameras and bags. They were walking in a bizarre manner to stay upright. They looked like a parade of freaks. The rain was coming at us sideways. The boat was tilting around like a top. Even the photographers, I barely looked at them because I had one project and that was: hang on. So the extra gringo, I did see him. I saw him leading the photographers, then I didn't see him. He was just gone.

I didn't wonder where he went at the time. I thought nothing about him at all. But later, when it was over, and the dolphin was saved and who cares, and we were saved, and a big meal was going on, food being passed down the table, and we had to use candles because the electric went off in the storm, somebody thought of him—maybe because a gringa walked by, a woman. It was strange because where did she come from? She walked by in the dark in a dress, carrying a little suitcase like a briefcase. She came over and asked some questions in English. Then she walked away and a few minutes later somebody said, Hey, was she talking about that gringo with the head? What happened to him? Nobody knew. The owner looked for him and the untrainer looked for him. I was the one who said it. I don't know how but I knew. I said, He went overboard.

I am sure I was right.

The dolphin, the gray of distant stars, a perfect form in the air. Like a pipe dream loosened from the mind and set free to make its own way. The animal was gone so fast one felt its silver body ghosting behind it.

If a man throws himself into water (or is thrown into it, although that's not what we're talking about) in the middle of an active storm, he won't last long. He has a heart-wrenching shock as soon as he hits the water, and if he isn't saved right away a few heady waves push him under, especially if he can only use one arm. He opens his mouth in shock and his lungs fill. Within a couple of minutes, he's sinking, but by then he isn't really human anymore. Yes, the humanity is gone that quickly. He is flailing a little but now it is a function of impulse and instinct. He is no longer suffering. He had only a minute or so of that when his head still rose above the water but even then the suffering was physical, did not resemble a thought construction such as: Quick, throw me a rope. I have made a mistake. Save my life.

Rain stained away the color from the scene but some drops caught the light and some of those drops caught Myers as he leapt and they lit him up like foil. He was the fastest heart-beating object on the scene at that moment. You might think he was the most urgent too, but he wasn't. All life is urgent.

The jump itself wasn't the wriggling of a fish caught in a net. For all his fussing around before, now he was calm and controlled. If you could slow time, he would look like a person poised in air, floating.

What can be said about this man?

He went after things that weren't his.

Not now. This time he went first, and who's to say the dolphin wasn't following *him*?

Myers shot down the avenue of air and into the water.

There was one bass thud, then one sparkle-splash. Both gone. Then the underwater roar, each body moving off in its own direction.

But before all that, before they set the dolphin free and were heroes or at least not villains for one day, before they saw Myers's wife coming through the sand, before he threw himself over the side and did not see the dolphin free, did not cheer, Myers took the filmmakers on their walk.

Where are those goddamn lazy filmmakers? the untrainer shouted over the storm.

I believe they're in the engine room, Myers said.

What are they doing in the godforsaken engine room for fuck's sake when I assume that all there is to film is out here?

I believe they're keeping the cameras dry.

What do they have goddamn underwater cameras for?

(Myers had forgotten they had underwater cameras.)

We spend all this, go through all this, so they can hide in the engine room and we get no publicity?

(It did seem they were going through a lot.)

Tell them to get their lazy, inexperienced asses out here.

Myers had already untied himself from the boat because he was going to throw himself over the side before the dolphin did but he thought he should follow the order first. It was then that Myers took the bravest walk of his life (if he didn't count the walk from coffee table to mother at ten months of age, his first steps, the bravest in light of what followed, naively brave, unless there is another kind, and if he didn't count the walk down the aisle, or...). Was he scared? He didn't want to die this way, fetching the lazy, inexperienced filmmakers. Or he didn't want to fail in his job, his fetching job, he wanted the thing, the animal, recorded, but he nearly did, nearly failed and died before he could fetch them and then go over.

The passageway was narrow and nothing but a piece of chain separated him from the air and the ocean. He inched his way across the deck while everyone else, who was tied down tight, stared in horror and awe—or maybe they didn't. Maybe no one watched. There was a lot going on. Or a few of them watched, who knows. It was like in cartoons or like descriptions in books. The ship heaved and spun. Myers almost flew off. He held on to the chain with his good arm and swung out over the bursting water, held on, not for his life, but for the lazy, stupid filmmakers, for the dolphin they would film, for the viewers who would flip past and glimpse a ship, a sea, a sky, an animal leaping to its freedom as they made their TV rounds and were moved to make a donation, and for his wife, whom he loved and who might see it and understand why he twice plunged to his death. He held on. The ship righted itself. He made it back onto the slippery, watery deck. He scrambled into the engine room.

You'd better go take pictures, said Myers to the lazy, inexperienced filmmakers, who were hugging the walls.

It's a hurricane, they said. No way.

He's out there throwing a fit.

The cameras. We'll ruin our cameras.

You have underwater cameras.

Do not.

But they stood there holding them, trying to put them behind their backs. Finally they had to admit the truth. They agreed to follow him back across the narrow passageway. Myers then took the second bravest walk of his life. He led the way, screaming back through the storm to the stupid, lazy, inexperienced filmmakers to hold on to the chain. Hold on to the chain! he screamed all the way back to the dolphin. But when he looked behind him, he saw that there were no filmmakers behind him and that he wasn't going to get to throw himself overboard. They had tricked him, hadn't followed. He'd have to go back and get them again.

Just then he saw them, coming around the corner, and he could tell the walk had harrowed them, had changed them forever. Myers had done this, had converted them once and for all. Each of them would henceforth be sailors or men who feared the sea. Their gravestones would one day reflect what this walk had done to them. They had made it, one throwing up all over his wet suit, another getting hit in the back by a can of soda thrown by a waiter. They all tied themselves to the deck. The boat tipped. The water hit their faces. They snapped photos. They filmed.

Everyone was watching them, the lazy, inexperienced filmmakers. Meanwhile Myers—outlaw, husband, hero, vacationer—stepped over the chain and jumped.

Acknowledgments

The author would like to thank the following people for their crucial assistance in the creation of this book: Eli Horowitz, Gary Lutz, Diane Williams, Clancy Martin, Christopher Miller, Elliott Stevens, Jordan Bass, Rebecca Curtis, David McCormick, Richard and Helene O'Barry, Matt Evans, Bob and Nancy Unferth, Katherine Colcord, and Rosalyn Olin Porte.

Grateful thanks also to the MacDowell Colony, the University of Kansas, and Bobst Library at New York University.

Chapter Seventeen originally appeared in a different form in *NOON*.

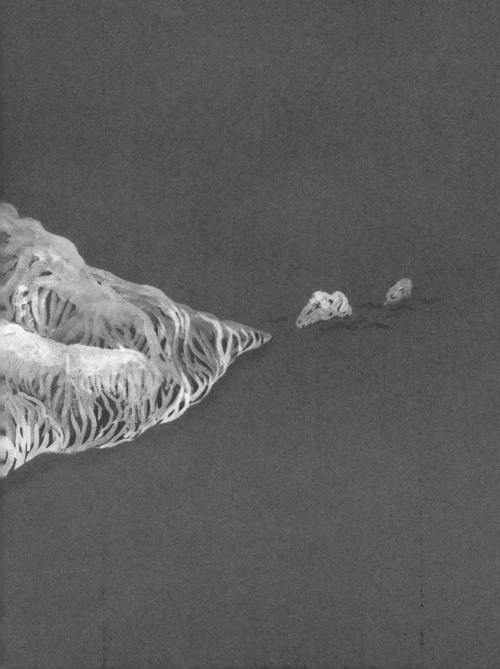